Please Don't Shoot An,
By Dave Newman

First Edition
ISBN # 978-0-9846198-2-5

Cover Illustration: Mike Turner
Cover Design and Interior Formatting: Mike Turner

Press and Press Contact Information:

World Parade Books
5267 Warner Avenue #191
Huntington Beach, CA
92649
www.worldparadebooks.com

Lori!

PLEASE DON'T SHOOT ANYONE TONIGHT

CHAPTER 1

I was in the back office of the paint store where I worked part-time. This was 1987. I was on the phone with my good friend Matt Williams. We were discussing our plans to rob the place. I was seventeen years old. Matt was seventeen. Matt had long hair and sometimes played in rock bands. I didn't. His girlfriend was pregnant. Mine was not. I wrote poems that I didn't show anyone. Matt could barely spell. We both thought Mike Tyson was the greatest boxer in the world.

It was nine o'clock. The store was empty. My manager—a fat man, fifty years old, a born-again Christian—was off somewhere with his wife. He did that. "Responsibility is important," he'd say, flip me the keys, and head to Dairy Queen.

I counted the money. I counted it again. The night deposit was twenty-three hundred, most of it checks and credit cards. The goal had been two thousand in cash. I touched the stack of twenties, then the tens. I touched the fives. The ones were piled a couple inches high with wrinkled bills. The coins were rolled, except for a few pennies.

Matt said, "So what do you think?"

I said, "Probably not."

"The gig is off?"

"The gig is definitely off."

"Maybe there will be another show soon?" he said.

This was code, not that we needed code, not that anyone at Pittsburgh Paints knew anything, but two thousand dollars was a lot of money, and we were sure we were being monitored. The phones had been tapped. The cops had been called. There were bugs. Maybe cameras. Everyone was a spy. I'd gotten a great review and a ten-cent raise the previous week, but that was part of it. The misdirection.

Crime was not new in my life. I shoplifted. I'd done it for years. I'd steal anything. At the mall, I put a fourteen carat gold necklace down the front of my pants and gave it to my mom for her birthday. I stole Izod shirts and Levis jeans. I stole perfume for girls I loved and girls I didn't. I could spot store security. I knew which ones didn't care. At gas stations, I filled up with unleaded, didn't pay, then drove backwards with the lights off until the manager couldn't see my license plate. I stole a six pack from a bar while buying a six pack. I drank a six pack, went back to the bar to buy a third six pack, and stole a fourth six pack and a forty ouncer of Schlitz. I was often drunk when I was stealing. Or stoned. Or both.

At work, I was sober. I was respectable and hard-working. My manager, the fat born-again Christian, went to church with my parents who were also born-again Christians, and even though I pretended my parents didn't exist, I knew they did, and I knew what would happen if I embarrassed them.

Matt said, "So."

I said, "Right. Probably next time."

I stood up and walked around the office. The office was tiny. It was a desk, a phone, a file cabinet. How-To manuals were stacked on a metal bookshelf. The beige carpet was brown with dirt and old paint the contractors tracked in. My stomach felt pumped with helium, like it was trying to float up and out of my body. I peeked out the door, but the store was still empty. The paint cans were stacked. The brushes hung neatly on the wall. Outside, the sun was down, but the lights above the parking lot hadn't kicked on.

Matt said, "What about a make-up show?"

I said, "Probably a Friday night show would be great."

"Any idea which Friday night?"

"Probably next Friday night, which would be a bummer because I have to work late."

Matt said, "Got it."

I hung up the phone.

What we'd just said, more or less, was this: the paint store makes its most money on Friday; Friday night would be a good night to rob this place; I don't work this Friday; I work next Friday; let's rob it then, if the money looks good. Then, what was implied: let's hook up later to get stoned and drunk.

I sat back down in the swivel chair. I felt relieved not to be robbing the paint store again. This was the third time we'd considered it, and the third time we'd backed out. The reasons were the same: we were short on money, eight hundred dollars wasn't enough; we didn't have a witness; my boss was eating ice cream with his three-hundred-pound wife; tonight, Marjorie, the assistant manager with a nervous habit who was supposed to witness the scam and validate the robbery and be scared, had called off with the sniffles.

I went back on the showroom floor with a broom and started to sweep. There was classical music on the speakers, and it sounded okay.

CHAPTER 2

A month ago, I'd been out with Matt. We were driving around. We were drinking beer. Matt had an old Nova. The Nova was a loud big-engined, freak mobile, the kind of car that drunk teenagers plow into trees and walk away from unscathed. It was Wednesday night, mellow. The roads were open. I'd worked until seven at the paint store and Matt had picked me up.

I was in my work clothes: brown jeans, a white oxford with paint stains on the cuffs, a brown-and-beige paisley tie, slightly frayed. I still had on my nametag, which we both thought was hilarious. Matt was in a black t-shirt. His hair, which he'd been growing since seventh grade, had finally reached his shoulders.

About three beers in, which was what it took for Matt to get buzzed, he said, "I'm having all kinds of problems here."

I said, "You want me to drive?"

"Not those kinds of problems."

"Like what?"

"Problems. Everything problems."

I said, "School?"

I didn't know what he was talking about. We weren't the kind of teenagers to have problems. We didn't care.

I said, "Your parents?"

He said, "Like Susan's pregnant."

I said, "You're fucking kidding?"

He said, "I wish."

Matt and Susan had been going out since early junior high, probably since Matt had started to grow his hair, a ridiculously long time for two juniors in high school. Susan was nice. I thought. I didn't know. She had a convertible Volkswagen. I'd slept with her older sister, a senior with a good personality and a bad complexion. Susan had a great complexion. She took honors classes. If I saw her in the halls, I always said hi or touched her in a friendly way. If I was having a party, or if I knew of a party, I invited Susan, sometimes before I even talked to Matt, to make her feel like she was part of something, like she wasn't just a girlfriend. She always thanked me and acted polite. She always offered two bucks to drink off the keg even though girls drank free.

Susan was, like all our girlfriends when we had girlfriends, a sort of distant sun that Matt retreated to when the beer was gone and the pot was smoked. She was nice and safe and fun to see a movie with when the house party you were going to attend got busted in advance.

Then, once, after I'd picked up Matt for a party, he said, "I have to swing by Susan's place." I didn't know why. I didn't ask. Maybe he needed money or he wanted to drop off an earring or he'd written her a love letter. We had beer, so I sipped a can of Old Milwaukee while Matt ran around back to the basement door. Ten minutes later, he was back, red-faced, his shirt untucked. He said, "That was a blowjob."

I said, "What was a blowjob?"

He said, "That," and motioned back towards Susan's house. He checked his zipper and adjusted his jeans. He grabbed a beer.

I said, "We just drove here so Susan could blow you?"

He said, "This party is probably going to be a bust. A bunch of dudes. Plus, Susan was feeling lonely. We're in love. Her mom wanted her to stay in tonight, so she wanted to see me for a couple minutes."

"So she could blow you?" I said.

He said, "Drive, man. Let's go. Her mom's gonna wonder why we're parked here. Peg it." He drank his beer. He said, "Besides, she loves it."

I said, "To blow you?"

"Yeah."

"You mean you like to be blown?"

"Both."

I said, "What'd you say after it was over?"

Matt said, "I don't know. I love you or something. I'll call tomorrow."

Blowjobs happened. They'd been happening since junior high. Girlfriends gave them because they loved you, and other girls, ones who weren't girlfriends, gave them to shut us up, because our begging was embarrassing, because they didn't know how to say no, because they loved to get attention, because their big sisters told them that boys loved blowjobs, whatever. Maybe, without even knowing it, they loved to give blowjobs. But no one, no female ever, none that I knew of, and this included Tabby—a thirty-five-year-old cokehead who lived in her dead parents' house and ate macaroni and cheese three nights a week and loved hanging out with high school boys—would just allow you to swing by and get sucked. There was protocol. There was kindness and conversation.

Except that Matt had just dropped in for some head.

A couple weeks later, when we were drinking in someone's basement, Matt told me that Susan liked to be fucked with a glass Coke bottle. I looked at him. He kept on.

"Not the whole bottle," he said.

I said, "Fuck you."

He said, "Seriously." He said, "Don't tell anyone, or she'll totally cut it out. I told Robbie she liked to finger herself in front of me and Robbie told everyone. I didn't get anything, not even a handjob, for a month."

I said, "But a Coke bottle?" I said, "Does that even feel good?"

Matt said, "Yeah. It's glass. I put it in the bathtub to warm it up."

"Skinny end or fat end?"

"Skinny end."

"I still don't believe you."

Matt said, "You'll see."

I already said the year: 1987. We lived in Western Pennsylvania. There was no internet. We had porn, in magazine and on videotape, but it was not easy to get. There was a story of a girl at another school who had taken a couple Spanish Flies and fucked herself to death on a gearshift, but mostly sex was still between two people and not objects. The Coke bottle story was fantasy, a wish, a prayer.

Matt said, "You'll see."

Then I saw.

A week later, he brought in a Polaroid, and there she was, Susan, face down on a pillow, ass up in the air, one hand on her own butt, the other between her legs, stuffing a green-tinted bottle, neck-first, up her twat. I was stunned. I was excited. I wanted a girlfriend who did things like this for me to take pictures of.

I said, "How did you get her to do this?"

Matt said, "It was her idea."

I said, "She must have some sort of brain damage, but in a good way."

I took another look at the Polaroid. I thought about Susan and every other girl I knew and Susan again.

I said, "She ever stick it up her own ass?"

Matt said, "Not yet," and laughed.

But that was then, at the beginning of our friendship, when we told secrets and bragged about sex. Now, in Matt's blue Nova, we were serious. We were talking about pregnancy, something that never sounded real, even though we were always pulling out and pretending it was safe.

Two years before, when I was in junior high, I thought I'd gotten a neighborhood girl, Lucy Arms, pregnant. We were lost and scared and clueless. Neither of us drove. Both our parents were religious. Lucy wanted me to stick a clothes hanger up her, not to give her an abortion, she said, but to get her period to come. I didn't do it. I would have, but I felt like we had time. I decided Lucy needed to run. Every night, we jogged two miles. Lucy was fat, and it was hard for her to keep up. She jiggled, and I imagined all that jiggling doing something inside her, making her unpregnant or less pregnant. Then she decided she would do sit-ups, one-hundred crunches every hour, until her period came. She supplemented the sit-ups by playing drums on her stomach with her fists. After a week, her period came. When I saw her in the hall, she shook my hand, smiled, and pressed a tampon wrapper into my palm.

But this was Susan we were talking about, not some fat junior high kid. Susan was smart and skinny, and her parents were lawyers, and her mom wouldn't let Susan try out for cheerleading because she thought it was degrading to women.

Now I drank off my beer. I turned to Matt and said, "So what's she want to do?"

He said, "I don't know. I don't have a clue."

For a guy who lived with confidence and energy and fun, for a guy whose life plan was to play bass and sing back-up for a heavy metal band, he looked folded out and ironed. He was pasty white with huge black circles under his eyes. His hands held the steering wheel at two and ten, just like we were taught in Driver's Ed. His arms were stiff as pencils. All that hair, which usually looked reckless, fit like a wig, like a disguise someone had placed on a scared teenager to hide the fear.

We headed east on Route 136, a winding backroad that cut through old farmland and new trailer parks. Matt took a hard right, down a short steep hill and past the Mail Pouch barn. The barn was decrepit now, the paint chipping from the rotting wood, the advertisement for chewing tobacco barely visible.

Matt said, "I should start chewing again. I could use something." Matt had quit Copenhagen because the snuff had eaten a small hole in his right cheek and he was worried that it would affect his singing. He touched his face. We knew a guy, a kid, fourteen years old, who had his lower lip removed.

Matt slowed the Nova. He backed us onto railroad tracks, far enough that the cops couldn't see us from the main road. We smoked dope here sometimes. Ate pills. Other times, we brought girls and parked. None of that felt possible anymore.

I said, "Okay."

He popped the gearshift into park and said, "I am so fucked."

I said, "How are you on money?"

He said, "Nothing. Beer money, that's it."

Matt's mom owned a catering business. One day a week, Matt worked there, making stuffed shells and cutting vegetables. During the summer, he nailed shingles and carried lumber for his dad's roofing business.

I said, "What happened to all that roofing money?"

He said, "It's idling right now."

"This piece of shit?"

"People like old Novas," he said. "They're expensive pieces of shit. They're like the poor man's Mustang." He said, "I should have bought a fucking Horizon like my dad said. I could have gotten a Horizon for half of what I paid for this fucking Nova."

He put his head against the steering wheel. His long hair fell across his face, and he looked as sad as anyone I had ever seen who wasn't about to be punched.

He said, "What am I gonna do?"

I wanted to say: abortion. It was an obvious answer, but for as often as I heard the word on TV and at church and during elections, I'd never known anyone to have one. I didn't even know what exactly went into an abortion. I knew there was a baby in there, and they, the abortion people, took it out, but I didn't know how, except that they didn't use a clothes hanger, which, as far as I could tell from stumbling on a magazine article, was one of the reason they legalized abortion in the first place—to keep women from hurting themselves.

I finally said, "She doesn't want it, does she?"

Matt said, "No." He said, "Yes." He said, "What kind of seventeen-year-old girl wants a baby? She wants a life and stuff."

"But she doesn't want an abortion?" I said.

"Of course she doesn't want an abortion. She doesn't want anything. She wants to cry all the time. It's the pregnant hormones or something. She's crazy."

I said, "How late?"

He said, "A couple weeks."

"We need to get you some money."

"I'm sorry to lay this on you."

He looked away and started to cry. It was not a lot, but the sounds filled the car, and I looked at the trees hiding the train tracks. The moon was out there, beyond the windshield. It was a slice of yellow, hanging over the barn. There were stars.

I said, "Pay attention," and I started. I talked and I made notes in my head. Matt listened. He wiped his face with his shirt. I sometimes backtracked to go over a point or change a detail. It was wisdom and music, even when it didn't make exact sense.

Matt said, "Are you making this shit up or did you have this planned out?"

I said, "Making it up."

He said, "You're a genius."

This, then, was our plan: rob Pittsburgh Paints. An abortion, I decided, was three hundred dollars. It could have been more or less, but three hundred sounded right. Matt would need additional money for the weekend. He couldn't just drop Susan off for an abortion, pick her up in an hour, and send her home like they'd been out for burgers. They would need a motel room and food and access to a video rental store. There'd be lies, of course, but that was almost always the truth about growing up.

"If we're gonna do this," Matt said, "you have to keep your share."

"I don't need it," I said, and I hadn't considered keeping any of the money, but now I wanted it. My share.

The paint store paid minimum wage. Two weekends a month, I worked at a slaughter house. Spring and Summer, I cut grass. Winter, I shoveled snow. I was always broke. If I wasn't broke, I thought I was. I hid money in my room, dug it out, spent it. I went back to work to make more. I sold paint. I cleaned blood off the killing floor. I ran with a lawnmower and dug snow until the shovel cracked on the ice.

My mom often cried about money. My dad worked construction and when a job ended, when the last wire had been plastered into a wall and the lights went on, my mom started crying and didn't stop until the union office secured my dad his next job. Then my mom would say, "It won't last," or, "We won't make it." Even now, with my dad working a good factory job, my mom would sometimes break and say, "They're going to pull out and go back to Germany."

She'd say, "Why would Volkswagen care about American workers?"

My dad's jobs. My mom's crying. It put money on my brain.

Now this: the opportunity to split a sack filled with cash. It was obvious, and I wondered why I hadn't thought of robbery the first time I'd opened the cash register at the paint store.

I said, "I don't want it. It's your money."

Matt said, "I'm not doing it if you don't take half. It'll be retarded."

"I don't want it."

"Then no way. We need another plan."

I said, "What other plan?"

He said, "Take the money." He said, "Seriously." He said, "Please."

My neighborhood was filled with truck drivers and factory workers and railroad employees and men on disability. I knew money was the bricks that built our houses. Thus, being a teenager and a moron, I pretended not to believe in money and treated it like a ghost. I often picked up checks for friends at restaurants, not because I was generous, but because I was embarrassed. My mom was worried. My dad was cheap. I didn't want that. Now, Matt was talking about splitting thousands of dollars, and I played it like pennies.

Finally, I said, "Look, I'll split it with you, but whatever extra you need, you can have. If you need more, it's yours."

"Deal," he said.

We went back to the plan. It would be an inside job. I'd be the connection. My job would be the set-up. I would make it look like an outside job.

Matt would be the outside guy. He would be the crook, the burglar. Those were the words I used: inside job, connection, set-up, outside guy, crook, burglar. I'd watched a lot of Humphrey Bogart movies with my dad, and I was sure I knew how to rob anything.

Matt said, "I'm not using a gun."

I said, "Of course you're not using a gun."

Every night at closing, someone, usually more than one person, walked the night deposit to the bank at the other end of the strip mall. The strip mall was shaped like an L. The bank was in the corner. It was dark there, set back from the other stores. The area was decent, working-class but without crime, and I'd never once been afraid, but the bank and the darkness would explain everything to the cops.

On Wednesdays, I worked with Marjorie, a nice but incompetent housewife who worked three shifts a week for something to do now that her kids were grown. Marjorie liked looking through wallpaper books. She liked her twenty percent discount. She'd been married right out of high school, immediately knocked up, and she'd never had a real job. With customers, she was fine, friendly and good at sales, but she was confused by the new cash registers. She couldn't place a special order. She couldn't find the special orders that had been placed. She took an hour to close when it took everyone else fifteen minutes. Marjorie would be our target. I liked Marjorie, and I didn't want anything to happen to her, but when asked to hand over the money she would hand over the money. She would be scared and compliant. Counting money at night often left her scared and compliant. She would sometimes be five hundred dollars off and near tears, and I'd find a calculator, take over, and easily balance the till.

Matt said, "What if she freaks out and screams?"

"Be fast," I said. "Have a line. Tell her it's a stick-up or whatever. Get the money and run. I'll pull her in the other direction like I'm super scared."

"This is too easy," he said. "We have to be missing something."

I said, "I think we've got it. All we need to do is ask for the money. You ask. You take. I'll be the witness. I'll tell the cops what happened. Exactly. So I don't even have to lie. This guy came up and asked for the money. We were scared. We gave him the money. He ran. We ran. That's it, Officer."

Matt said, "Unbelievable." He sat up and found a beer. He popped the top and drank. He looked like someone had shoveled fuel back into the engine of his body. He said, "I can't tell you how much I appreciate this."

"I know," I said, though I easily could have thanked him, though I easily could have said, "I really appreciate this." This: the chance to become a criminal. This: the chance to pay for an abortion. That's how it was, being seventeen. Things spun backwards and got confused.

Matt said, "I'm serious. Thank you."

I said, "You're welcome."

He stuck out his fist. I touched it with mine.

He said, "I need to go to sleep. I'm fucking exhausted. I've been walking around with this for days and not telling anyone. I'm just so tired." He yawned out his last words.

I said, "Let's get out of here."

He said, "I can't." He said, "I'm sorry. I have to lie down. Give me fifteen minutes and I'll be fine." He reached for the lever and the entire bench seat, his side and mine, reclined. He said, "Twenty minutes, tops," and closed his eyes.

I said, "Sure," and tried to find a comfortable way to sit up on a reclined seat.

I turned on the radio. I turned off the engine. There was beer, and I didn't have to be home for a couple hours. I popped another can.

Within seconds, Matt was snoring. Fifteen minutes passed. Then thirty. I knew he needed sleep. My mom said that sometimes on the weekend when I slept in, "You probably needed the sleep." An hour passed. Matt looked peaceful. Doing nothing, just letting Matt sleep, felt like something. Thirty more minutes passed. I finished all the beer. The radio died. I hit the button. Nothing happened. I tried the engine. The key turned and the engine wheezed and stopped.

Matt sat up. He said, "How long was I out?" He had drool on his chin.

I said, "An hour. Maybe more."

He said, "I think the battery's dead."

I said, "Shit, I'm drunk."

He said, "Let's go. Rhino lives right down the road. He'll have jumper cables."

I said, "Who the fuck is Rhino?"

We stood outside the car. I felt wobbly, but in a good way. Matt rubbed his face and fixed his hair. He asked if I was okay to walk. I said I was. Neither of us moved. We were on the train tracks. The ties were rotten. The rails were rust. The whole thing should have crumpled, but trains rolled through here once or twice or three times a day.

Matt said, "But isn't it just too weird? The paint store has been in the same shopping center for like twenty years, and nothing's happened."

"Yeah," I said. "And now it does."

Matt headed down the tracks. I had to piss. I stepped into the woods and leaned against a tree. I unzipped my pants. Matt called my name. I called back.

CHAPTER 3

At the paint store, I called my mom and told her I was meeting friends. We were going to hang out and study for the Pre-SATs. She said, "On a school night?" and I said, "Yeah," and she said, "Oh, okay." We were going through a good period. She left me alone, and I didn't get caught doing terrible things. It was simple and easy, and I never knew why we weren't able to maintain this relationship for more than a few weeks at a time.

I turned off the lights in the stockroom and tucked the money bag under my arm. I locked the front door and walked the sidewalk to Irwin Bank. I made the drop. I checked the drop box to see if the money had fallen into the bank. It had. The plaza was empty. I imagined the robbery. It was easy, but not as easy as the first night we'd talked about it.

I hopped into my VW Diesel and headed east to meet Matt at a party. The ride was twenty minutes. Any longer and I would have used my fake ID to get a forty of Colt .45 or Old English. Often I raced backroads with a beer bottle between my legs and nothing else but a destination and the desire to catch a buzz before I arrived.

CHAPTER 4

There were eight other people at the party. Four of the kids were, I thought, around twelve. They passed a bag filled with glue or some chemical that would get you stoned. They tipped over like dominoes then sat up and passed the bag again. They were on the floor, in a circle, not much more than a pile of bodies with smiles and glossed-over eyes.

Matt, forcing down his second Old Milwaukee pounder, said, "Let's not reduce ourselves to that, okay?"

"Not on a school night," I said.

I was on my fourth Old Mil. I hated Old Mil but it was cheap. Cold, it would have been tolerable. Warm, from being hidden for a week under a pine tree in a small forest by Matt's house, the taste was sheet metal and urine.

Matt took a sip and gagged.

I said, "This shit is undrinkable."

He said, "What if they didn't put alcohol in this stuff?"

I said, "We'd be drinking Coke." Then, "How'd you hear about this party?"

"This?" he said and looked around to make sure we were at a party. "My neighborhood connection told me about it."

"Not a good connection."

"Yeah really," he said. "At least the tunes are decent."

Four guys were in the living room, watching some sort of heavy metal video show on MTV. Wasp was on, and it was hideous. Blackie Lawless was on the TV screen, in full goth make-up, with a knife attached to his cod piece. A cod piece was bad enough, but to have a knife sticking out like a violent sharp cock was disgusting, and my favorite band was Motley Crue and Motley Crue was mostly famous for taking drugs and dying and being revived.

Matt leaned back on the kitchen table like he was about to boost himself up and use it for a chair when one of the legs collapsed. There was a crack then a metal ping as the leg dropped to the floor. Matt jumped away and the table wobbled but never actually tipped. In a place like this, three legs were all you needed.

One of the glue-huffers, shocked out of his stupor, said, "Dude," like his voice was in slow motion, like he might have cared that another thing in this place had fallen apart.

Another huffer said, "Not a problem. It happens all the time," and went to stand up and fix the table, but he couldn't get his legs uncrossed.

Matt ignored the kids and said, "Why the fuck does this shit happen to me?" He looked over his own shoulder and grabbed at his ass to see if a nail or screw had cut through his jeans.

I said, "Nice," and raised my beer.

Matt said, "I probably have tetanus."

I looked around the kitchen. It was a place where you could catch something. We were in a tiny apartment in Youngwood. Apartments were, I'd assumed, for college people and people who didn't go to college and delivered pizzas and smoked too much weed. The availability of houses, many of them dumps, in Western Pennsylvania was such that I couldn't imagine how bad off a family had to be to end up crammed inside five rooms that weren't attached to a garage.

My own house, even though my dad often remodeled, was small and average, neat but lacking in character. The outside was red brick. The inside looked exactly like our neighbor's house and his inside looked identical to the next house down. Our house had a new bathroom and half a gameroom (with carpeting but without padding underneath). A few neighbors had two-story houses with nicer landscaping and one guy decorated his lawn with car parts from junkers, but everyone was working-class, striving for something better, satisfied with what they had already earned.

This apartment was not that. The carpet smelled like dog. The linoleum was peeling back. The shower curtain in the bathroom was covered in black mold. I didn't know anyone who lived like this, but it neither surprised nor bothered me. Tomorrow, the party could have been at a mansion in Wendover, and there might have been an indoor swimming pool or a Jacuzzi in the bathroom, and that would have been as acceptable as brown water running from the kitchen sink like it was doing at a trickle right now.

Matt said, "What do you think?"

I said, "About this?"

"Yeah."

"You smashing the table or the party in general?"

He said, "Both."

I said, "Makes me want to go home and study."

"Fuck it," he said. "It'd be worth it if we'd pulled something off, but this is a dud."

I said, "I wish we had a grand apiece in our pockets."

Matt said, "Tell me."

I poured the rest of my beer into the dented kitchen sink and turned the brown water on full. I shook the can and set it down on the brown countertop that was chipping away so that the pressed wood was starting to show.

I said, "Whose place is this?"

Matt said, "Mary Wilson."

"Who?"

"I've known her since second grade. One of those glue-huffers is her little brother. I don't know where she is. She's dating a biker who's forty or something."

"Where's her folks?"

He said, "Vegas."

I said, "I hope they win."

He said, "They won't."

I looked into the living room. I think I was looking for girls. There were none. I was bored and hungry.

I said, "You want to eat?"

Matt said, "Let me check," and pulled out his wallet, a black leather thing attached to a chain that hooked to a belt loop. He said, "Fourteen bucks."

I had more than that. Back at the paint store, when I realized the burglary was off, I charged a customer for a gallon of paint and didn't ring it in the register. I handed the woman a receipt that another customer had forgotten. I hit some buttons. I made change for a twenty. It was a scam I sometimes pulled. I pocketed seventeen dollars.

Matt said, "Let's eat." Then, "I need to call Susan first. If I call after eleven, her mom gets angry or her dad wants to talk."

"Let me piss," I said and headed to the bathroom.

What I meant was: let me go check the medicine cabinet for pills.

The summer before, while visiting my brother at college, one of his friends had taken me party-hopping. The friend, Donnie, was a surfer dude on the verge of failing out. He was a nice guy, prone to say stuff like, "Narly," and "Rad," and, "Wanna smoke some cool bud," exactly like Spicolli in *Fast Times at Ridgemont High*, only we were at Slippery Rock University, nowhere near a beach and some tasty waves. Donnie and I went from frat house to college apartment to dorm room, even once to a single-wide trailer, and everywhere we went, he cleaned out the pills in the medicine cabinet. He took prescription drugs. He took over-the-counter allergy medication (which he insisted was speed). He took vitamins (for the day after). He swigged from bottles of cough syrup and said, "Codeine," like it was a flavor. He took everything and stuffed it all down his flowered beach shorts. He didn't offer me anything, but I liked being there, and it seemed a skill worth acquiring. Back home, at high school parties, I started to steal my own small pharmacy, valium and cough syrup and seconal and benzies. I took some and gave some away and took some more and gave some away and stole some more and ate those and ran out.

In this apartment with holes punched into the plaster walls, I was sure there was a bottle or lots of bottles filled with narcotics.

The doorknob on the inside of the bathroom door was off so I had to latch a hook into an eyehole to keep it shut. I turned on the water, and it was less brown as it poured from a rusty faucet. The mirror on the medicine cabinet had been smeared with nail polish then half-cleaned so pinkish streaks slashed up my reflection. As I opened the door, I coughed to cover the sound. Inside, it was empty. Completely. The meds were gone. The shelves were gone. No razors, no shaving cream. No make-up. No fingernail clippers. I closed the door and didn't bother coughing. I flushed and spit in the toilet as the water swirled away.

Back in the kitchen I nodded to Matt.

He said, "You ready?"

I said, "Let's go."

We stepped onto the front porch, a sort of concrete slab that connected all the front-facing apartments. It was littered with living room furniture and milk crates filled with blankets and other bedding. The glass had been knocked out of the porch light but the bulb still burned, so we could see our way down the cracked steps.

When we were far enough away, Matt said, "What'd you get?"

I said, "Absolutely nothing."

"Come on," he said. "Junkies live there."

"Yeah, well," I said. "They've eaten all the good stuff or taken it to Vegas."

Matt said, "Unbelievable."

I was parked behind his Nova. The next parked car was a block away. I unlocked the door and my inside light lit up the night.

Fourth Street, the main drag, the street with the gas station and the Dairy Queen and the cheap motel, was empty of traffic. Youngwood was a small town, a few miles east of the Volkswagen factory. It was filled with dive bars that served minors, Italian restaurants that didn't, churches, old schools that had been converted to rec centers, rec centers that had been closed because of the dwindling population, and old houses, some as large as mansions, others average and common, and some held together with black shingles and rotting wood.

I spit on the sidewalk. I cleared my throat and did it again.

I said, "I can't get that warm Old Milwaukee taste out of my mouth."

Matt said, "It'd be easier to get wrecked on pills."

"I wish I would have scored some."

"You should have checked the medicine cabinet in the back bedroom. I bet that's where they keep their stash."

Then Matt pulled a dirty orange medicine bottle from each of his front pockets and shook the bottles like tiny maracas.

I said, "You really are a trained professional."

He said, "I am. I really am."

The sights and sounds of the drugs energized me. I didn't even want to do them, but just having some for when I needed them made me feel comfortable and less worrisome, like the pills were money remade into tiny narcotic bubbles.

Matt said, "The labels look like they were soaked in water, but one's definitely vikes. I don't know about the other."

He handed me a bottle. I turned the overhead light back on. With my thumb, I popped the cap and dumped a couple pills into my palm. They were big, with a split down the middle for an easy break, and a delicate blue in color.

Matt said, "What do you think?"

I said, "I don't know. That's a pretty blue."

He said, "It's like candy."

I said, "It's probably heartburn medicine."

"Let's find out," he said.

He took one of the pills from my palm and tossed it into his mouth. Once the pill was on his tongue, he didn't know what to do. There was nothing to drink in the car, we'd dumped our beers, and the pill was too fat to go down dry. I capped the medicine bottle. I smiled and turned off the dome light. Matt was having a moment. I had them, too. It was that split-second delay between the impulse to be cool and the reality of coolness. The impulse was to randomly take whatever pill you could get. The reality was choking down a marble when your mouth was dry as summer dirt from having pounded two cheap beers.

Matt opened the door and spit the pill on the street. He turned back to me, held up his finger, then exploded with cough. He opened the door and spit again. He revved up his throat and did it three or four more times.

I said, "Are you stoned? Because you look stoned."

He said, "It's like there's glue in my mouth."

He looked in the rearview mirror, and started to clean up his tongue with his hand.

I said, "You really are rock n' roll."

He said, "You really are a dick."

I started the Volkswagen and headed towards New Stanton, a turnpike exit only a few miles down the road. New Stanton had bad food and bright lights advertising buffets for all the truck drivers to see from the interstate. It was almost eleven o'clock. I didn't have to be home, but if I came home before midnight it counted for something.

I said, "What about McDonalds?"

Usually we ate at Eat N' Park, a local diner, but hungry men coming off second shift would soon be jamming up the buffet.

Matt said, "McDonalds is fine. Susan is probably sitting by the phone, getting pissed that I haven't called." He said, "I really need something to drink. Like a Coke. I feel like I just painted my tongue with chalk dust."

"You did," I said. Then, because one of us needed to mention it, I asked about Susan, if anything had changed.

"Same," Matt said.

"She still has the same ideas?" I said.

Ideas wasn't the right word, but it stood in.

He said, "Not really. I don't know. She's looking for me to take care of everything. I don't know what to do. Her parents are fucking lawyers. Doesn't that mean she should know something? My dad roofs fucking houses." He said, "I need some money or none of this matters." He said, "I haven't even been thinking about it. Or I'm trying not to. We'll either get the money from the paint store or we won't. That's all I know. Susan doesn't even know that."

Matt stretched out. He took a breath. He looked angry but contained.

He said, "She doesn't know anything. All she knows is how to fuck. That's it. She's a smart girl with good parents and some money, and she thinks fucking is the answer to everything. I don't even feel like it. Fucking's what we did to get here. But with Susan, everything is suck and fuck. I look at her, and she looks like the other girls in the halls at school, and then we get alone, and it's suck and fuck." He paused. He said, "I don't even know what I'm saying. Just that we've been fucking like nothing's up. I keep hoping her period just shows up."

"It seems unreal," I said.

"It is unreal," he said. "We've fucked like nine million times and nothing. Now, all of a sudden, she thinks she's pregnant."

Matt pulled the rearview mirror towards the passenger seat and looked at his mouth, his tongue, his face. I told him to relax. He said he was. He said he couldn't. I moved the mirror back. We passed his mom's catering business. We passed the Three Rs Bar where we sometimes scored six packs and old men drank their pensions away.

I wondered if we were to the point where we needed to get Susan running and doing sit-ups. I was sure there was a drug somewhere, legal or not, that would take care of this. If Susan took enough aspirin, and drank something else, vodka or beer or grain alcohol maybe, surely it would take care of what was growing inside her. There were recipes for everything. But we weren't being creative. We needed brain power. Susan needed to start wishing against her insides. We all did.

I said, "Did she take a pregnancy test yet?"

He said, "No. She's afraid to go to her doctor. She's afraid her doctor will get her mom involved and the whole thing will go to shit."

"What about a home pregnancy test?"

"Do those even work?"

I said, "Yeah." I said, "I don't know." I said, "Why wouldn't they?"

He said, "Because you can buy them in the tampon aisle. It just seems a little obvious or something."

I said, "Tampons work."

Matt said, "You want to steal one?"

I said, "Is there a twenty-four grocery around here?"

"There'll be something in New Stanton."

We kept on down the road. Matt flipped around on the radio. The music we liked never made it to the radio. Another minute passed, and the road opened up and became I-70. An old Elton John song came on. It was a wimpy one with lots of fancy piano. Matt hit the button.

He said, "I don't care if I ever hear another song on the radio again." He said, "Does McDonalds have the cheeseburger special going on? The last time I was there, some kooky manager tried to tell me it ended at four o'clock or something. You don't end a cheeseburger special right before dinner. That makes no fucking sense."

I said, "I'll buy you a cheeseburger."

He said, "Fuck it. I'll probably just get some fries." He said, "I hope they have fresh fries. We should demand fresh fucking French fries."

Matt was so far into his own problems that the original problem was beginning to disappear and everything else—the radio, McDonalds—was becoming the focus. I wasn't that deep—I couldn't have gotten that deep into someone else's life—so it was easy for me to cruise along and think of solutions. If not solutions, then clues.

What I didn't say but wanted to was this: is Susan showing? Is her belly sticking out? Do her clothes still fit? I trusted a belly more than a missed period. Girls missed periods for lots of reason—stress or they got too skinny or they just weren't regular—but a belly, a big hard pregnant belly, was undeniable.

I started to say, "How's Susan look naked?" but that was wrong, but then I didn't know what was right or if there was a right.

Matt said, "There!" and sat up straight and started to roll down the window.

"There where?" I said.

"Those two chicks," he said and pointed towards a sports car parked at the gas station I had just rolled by.

I said, "Who are they?" but I was already turning around.

CHAPTER 5

Matt said, "Donna and that other one, whoever she is."

"Who's Donna?"

"Some chick I know. She's cool She's old."

Matt talked and pointed at the place I was already heading.

He said, "She's thirty or thirty-five or forty or something. But completely cool. I used to go over and smoke grass at her house all the time. She was the secretary for my dad's company, then she went back to school and became a dental assistant. Or she takes x-rays. I don't know exactly. Her tits are huge."

I said, "Speak clearly, I don't understand what you mean by huge tits."

Matt said, "Don't joke. This is serious."

"I am serious," I said.

"No," Matt said. "I mean serious."

I said, "Do I not look serious?"

Matt didn't look at me. He said, "I don't know." He said, "Be serious."

But serious was our problem. Teachers and bosses and parents all said it, serious, be serious, seriously, and all those years of confusion had taken us, and now we didn't know the difference between getting a "D" in English and driving into a concrete wall. Overdoses looked like fashion statements. Fashion statements were overdoses. It was all the same party. Everything looked like a disaster, except disasters which looked like success stories, but then our success stories often felt like disasters.

And then, like now, it didn't.

The beer showed up. The chance to get laid. Drugs were plentiful. The sickness, the future, looked less tragic. Susan's pregnancy wasn't going to go away tonight, and these women weren't going to be here tomorrow. The earth shifted. We moved further down hill.

I pulled into the parking lot. The lot was paved but filled with potholes. Mounds of asphalt bounced my car. I pulled up, but not too close to the Firebird. It was a nice car, red and shiny under the gas station lights. A giant bird was painted on the hood.

I turned to Matt and said, "Give me a pill."

"Which one?"

"A vike," I said. "Don't be a dipshit."

"Two seconds," he said. He finished rolling down the window. He said, "Donna. Hey, Donna. It's me. It's Matt."

Donna's friend, the one without a name, was in the Firebird, but Donna stopped what she was doing and looked to see who was yelling her name. I couldn't tell her looks, but she had a sexy walk, and she was dressed, I thought, like a waitress.

Donna said, "Matt? Matt Williams?" She said, "Are you kidding me? What are you doing out at this hour, you big pussy? I thought you had school tomorrow."

Matt said, "Never," and leaned out the window.

I knew good things were about to happen, some happy disaster, but I was still surprised when Donna leaned down and kissed Matt full on the mouth. Then, like nothing, she stopped and started talking like Matt was her best friend. It was intimate and a little disappointing. I'd thought, for some reason, Donna was mine. I leaned back and tried to see her friend.

Matt said, "You working? How's work?"

"Work," Donna said, like the word itself was an answer and the answer wasn't worth repeating. She shook her head and laughed and said, "Work didn't work out."

"Work didn't work out?" Matt said.

All I could see was Donna's tits and her chin.

She said, "Working in a doctor's office did not work out. It was seriously stupid, and the doctor was always checking out my tits."

"They're great tits," Matt said.

"Not on the job they're not," Donna said.

I moved for a better view. Donna had on a tight yellow t-shirt with a black submarine sandwich silk-screened across the front. She stood up and leaned back down. I leaned forward then back. She had sexy lips and too much make-up. She had a man's chin. Her tits were big and solid. A small belly hung over her jeans. I tried to imagine her ass.

Only a year ago, I'd quit football, and I still lifted weights. I could have pressed Matt, who was built like Axl Roses on a coke bender, over my head. It was ridiculous that Matt would end up with Donna. She was too much. He was too little. They kissed again.

Matt said, "So where's the party?"

Donna said, "My place. You coming?"

That was easy. I looked at Matt, at the back of his head, which was all I could see, and wondered if I should grow my hair long.

"You got beer?" he said.

"Two sixers, I think. Should I get more?"

Matt said, "There's you and me and your friend and mine."

"Pammy doesn't drink," she said.

"Danny does," I said, leaning over and saying my own name.

Donna squatted down and rested her elbows on the passenger-side window ledge. I waved and she smiled and waved back. She had brown hair in a ponytail, and she was dark from the tanning bed. Her face was okay, plain but nice, tired. There was the hint of a mustache, but it had been bleached.

She said, "Aren't you a cutie?"

I said, "Could I get one of those kisses?"

She said, "It might hurt your friend's feelings."

I said, "He doesn't have feelings."

Matt said, "It's true. I don't have feelings. You can give him a kiss."

She said, "Pammy might get jealous."

Donna turned and waved to Pammy. Pammy, from behind the windshield, waved back and smiled. I waved so hard I probably looked like a spaz.

Donna said, "I'm gonna go grab another six. Meet me back at my place."

I lifted my hips and went for my wallet. I didn't know if Donna had money, but I was happy to pay and, I figured, a woman with a hoagie printed across her chest would appreciate a man who was willing to treat.

I said, "Get two six packs of anything not Old Milwaukee."

She took the money and said, "Milwaukee's Best?"

She turned and headed for her bitchin' Firebird. From behind, she looked great. Her jeans were painted on, and, in the style of the day, rode the whole way up her ass-crack.

I turned to Matt and said, "Tell me you've been tapping that."

"Never."

"You're lying."

He said, "I wish. She gets drunk and kisses me up and that's it."

"What about tonight?"

"Let's hope," he said.

"What about Pammy?" I said.

"I don't know Pammy. Pammy's a stupid fucking name."

"I don't care about her name," I said.

CHAPTER 6

We stood on the front porch, in the dark, waiting while Donna looked for her keys. Matt was right beside Donna, and I was a few feet behind them, holding hands with Pammy. Pammy's hands were sweaty and her grip on my fingers was tight.

Donna said, "Fuck me. I do this all the time."

Matt said, "Let's see that purse," and he started digging through and pulling out an assortment of junk and sunglasses and old tissues. He said, "Is all this make-up necessary?"

Donna said, "It is if I want to keep getting hot young guys like you, you little smartass." She grabbed for her purse and took it back.

Matt said, "That thing's a suitcase."

Pammy said, "I carry ID and cash. That's all a girl really needs."

Donna, digging deeper and sitting junk on the window ledge, said, "And you mooch my make-up and cigarettes all night, you whore."

"Oh whore this," Pammy said, and flipped Donna off.

Donna, without looking up, said, "Are you flipping me the bird?" A compact fell to the concrete and she said, "Shit a brick."

Pammy said, "You are one clumsy bitch."

Donna bent for the compact and gave Pammy the finger.

It was obvious these women cared deeply for each other. Everything they said, every joke and obscene gesture, indicated a deep and lasting friendship. I wondered if Matt and I would end up like this, best friends, standing outside an apartment with two young girls who were half our ages. I thought we would. Our ages would change. Our habits would stay the same.

Donna said, "Where the hell are you, keys?"

Matt said, "I'm gonna throw a chair through that window in about two seconds if you don't find those fucking keys."

"Really," I said. "We have to be up for school tomorrow," and everyone laughed.

Pammy and I gently bumped shoulders.

Two minutes before this, when we'd parked in the alley behind the apartment, I'd walked up to Pammy and said, "Hi, I'm Danny."

She smiled and said, "Hey, I'm Pammy."

I said, "Pammy and Danny."

She said, "Like the TV show."

I said, "Hey, yeah, that's right," but I didn't know the show.

She said, "Well, sort of."

I said, "Sort of, yeah, exactly."

She said, "You're funny."

Pammy was prettier than Donna, but she was also thin as a guitar string. We were under the streetlights, and every time she turned away, I sneaked another look at her body. It was bright enough to see Pammy was beautiful, and at least as old as Donna, maybe older.

Pammy said, "I like your tie."

There it was: my paisley tie. Next to my tie was my nametag. My front shirt pocket was stuffed with a small notebook and two Bic pens. My belt was made of vinyl, and my shoes were splattered with a rainbow of colors. I lifted the tie and shrugged.

I said, "Gabes," which was a local store that sold factory rejects. "Two bucks."

She said, "I love Gabes."

I said, "Everybody loves Gabes."

She said, "I had to cut this tank-top and re-stitch the shoulder strap because it was so crooked, but it was on sale for, like, ten for a dollar."

She lifted the strap. It looked very straight.

I said, "You're a regular seamstress."

She said, "I sew when I get bored. My grandma taught me."

We kept talking. I took Pammy's hand. She held on. I said some funny things, trying to be charming. Pammy laughed. Mostly I stared. The more I stared, the less skinny she looked. I'd been expecting Donna's twin, another woman backed with curves, but now, as we talked, I could see the muscles. Pammy wasn't skinny. She was fit. Her arms were ripped. Her chest, which was almost devoid of tits, was lightly puffed with muscle. Her forearms had a few veins rippling through them, and so did her hands, but she made all of this, somehow, feminine.

I said, "Do you exercise? Like do aerobics?"

She said, "I used to. I still do sometimes. I jog a lot now."

"Jogging's good."

"I eat a lot of tuna."

"I love tuna," I said.

She said, "The mayo is terrible for you."

I said, "I hate mayo."

Matt turned and said, "I hope you two aren't talking about tuna salad."

Donna said, "Really. No talking about anything that can go on a sub. I live with that."

Pammy said, "The thought police." She lifted my hand. She said, "You need some sun. Look how white you are."

I said, "We should go to the beach."

She said, "The beach," and held our hands to her chest and sighed. She had the color. I couldn't imagine how many sessions she spent in a tanning bed. Even her lips, which were painted a brownish red, looked tan. She must have sensed me staring because she said, "My hair's a mess."

I said, "No it's not," and it was true.

Pammy's hair was the kind that didn't mess up. It was straight, shoulder-length, with bangs. No curl. No style. Her eyes were big and brown, and her eyelashes long and curled, but not fake, not like the spiders I'd seen crawling off the middle-aged women who shopped for wallpaper at the paint store. Pammy had lines, but the lines looked like experience, like sex.

I said, "I am so in love with you."

She laughed and said, "Already?"

I said, "From the second I saw you sitting in that badass car."

"Well," she said. "That's flattering." Then, laughing, "I hope my husband doesn't mind. I think he may still be in love with me, too."

"That guy?" I said. "Come on. That guy is a chump."

"That is true," she said.

I leaned in and kissed her. It wasn't a full-on French kiss, but our mouths were open and I touched her tongue with the tip of mine. A second later, she stopped. I tried again, but she sort of dodged my lips.

She said, "Okay, big guy, we're out in the streets here."

Donna said, "I knew you two would hit it off."

Now, minutes later, she put the key in the lock and said, "Finally." She stepped inside and said, "Home sweet fucking home."

Matt said, "Hey, new walls."

Donna said, "You like that?"

"Purple and green, yeah."

"I just painted."

Pammy cleared her throat in a dramatic way.

Donna said, "We. Pammy and I just did it. Thank you, Miss Pammy."

Pammy said, "What do you think?"

I said, "It's great. You should be an artist," and I didn't say anything about the party, that I'd only been at one other apartment in my life, and that was an hour ago, and the place smelled like an armpit and looked like a hillbilly tooth.

Pammy said, "At least someone appreciates me."

"I do," I said.

I appreciated Pammy. I loved the apartment. The living room had two purple walls and two green walls. The kitchen, which was tiny, was filled with white cabinets that had little guitars stenciled along the edges. On the fridge was a picture of Jimmy Page, cut neatly from a magazine. Jimmy Page wore a bad velvet suit. He was covered in sweat and shredding on his guitar. The picture was held up with four magnets shaped like a guitar, a bass, a drum set, and a microphone. Donna flicked on the lights, but almost nothing happened, just a few track lights burning slightly above dim. By the TV, I noticed some bootlegged rock concerts on video. One was the Rolling Stones. Another was Deep Purple. One video was labeled with smeared marker I couldn't make out.

Donna said, "You giving yourself a tour?"

I said, "I like it. This is a cool place."

She said, "Cool. Thanks."

It was no wonder this woman dug Matt. He probably showed up drunk one night, guitar case in hand, threw down a couple funky bass lines, flipped his rock n' roll hair, and appeared as a vision to a woman who was still worshipping Led Zeppelin years after the drummer had puked himself to death.

I picked up a purple throw, folded it, and placed it neatly on a fuzzy green chair. I hadn't known this was acceptable adult living. My parents had an oil painting of the Last Super. They had a framed lighthouse, done in water colors. They had a pair of praying hands, made from plaster, on the knick-knack counter. We had a knick-knack counter.

Donna had a Jim Morrison blanket covering her living room window. She had a Janis Joplin clock. Her phone was a giant plastic Mickey Mouse.

My dad liked Frank Sinatra and big band stuff. My mom like The Bill Gaither Trio. We didn't have beer in the fridge.

Donna moved to the stereo and punched some buttons. The Rolling Stones came on. I didn't recognize the song, but the riff was undeniable.

Donna said, "We need to freshen up," and both women started for the bathroom.

Matt said, "Where's that beer?"

Donna said, "Shit, the car."

I said, "Did you lock the door?"

Donna said, "Of course I did," and went for her big purse, which was on the kitchen counter, right next to a Mick Jagger bobble-head.

Matt opened the fridge.

He said, "There's plenty here," and pulled out four bottles of Miller.

Pammy politely declined. Donna took a beer then set it back down while she messed with her purse. Matt handed me two bottles. I popped the cap on one and started to chug. I tilted the bottle back, and I was sure everyone would love me. Pammy touched my stomach in an affectionate way as she walked by, then held her hand there as my belly filled up. I finished the beer. Everyone laughed.

Pammy said, "Did you drink that whole thing?"

I looked at the empty bottle and said, "No."

She said, "My god."

The women moved towards the bathroom. It looked tiny in there, a sort of pink closet. I imagined them taking turns peeing while they made plans to give us sex. I opened the second beer and tried to down that but it was a struggle. Donna said something to Pammy in a whisper. My stomach felt like I'd tried to swallow the room. I closed my eyes and burped, but not loud enough to be obnoxious. I looked at Matt. He opened his beer. He held up a finger, meaning: wait. When the bathroom door closed, we exploded. I tried to quiet my laughter, but I couldn't. Matt covered his mouth and coughed until I settled down.

In a whisper, I said, "Dude, this is the way I dream it every night with my pud in my hand." Then

I said, "This is—" and I couldn't think of the word so I shouted, "Awesome!"

He sssh-ed me then said, "You fucker, yours is hotter than mine."

Matt raised his hand. I reached up for a high-five, but we ended in a clasp. The clasp became a bump. The bump turned into a hug. I spilled some of my beer. Matt grabbed a dish towel and wiped it up. Everything calmed. Then we exploded with laughter. Then we pulled back on our voices like they were signs that needed to be rolled up.

I went right up to Matt's ear and said, "Tell me you never fucked Donna."

"Never," he said. Then, barely audible, "We dry hump."

"Dry hump?"

"But she's never walked up and necked with me in public before. She usually gets freaked out because of my age."

I said, "Did you see Pammy's lips?"

He said, "You have to get head."

The bathroom door opened. Before we could pretend not to be talking about blowjobs, Donna bolted for the bedroom. The bedroom was only a few short steps across the small hallway, but Donna moved like a short stop gunning for second base. Her footsteps were rapid-fire across the carpet. She was laughing, and it sounded like she dove for the bed and the bed bounced and slammed into the wall.

Donna said, "Whoops!"

From the bathroom, Pammy said, "Clumsy bitch."

I leaned towards Matt and said, "Did you see that?"

He said, "Was that a nightie?"

I made a confused gesture with my beer bottle. I didn't know exactly what a nightie was. Victoria's Secret was a mail order service. I'd seen JC Penney's catalog, but it was nothing like the purple and black outfit that had just jiggled by. This was a bustier or a teddy, or some other lingerie I'd glanced at in porn and couldn't name. This was the kind of thing hookers wore in old Westerns, sans feathers, while they hammered shots at the saloon and the cowboys worked up a thirst out on the range.

I waited for Pammy to come out and I wondered if she would do the same thing, be dressed the same way. For all I knew, all adult women, the ones who weren't married and stuck at home sick and worrying about their teenage children, fucked in lingerie. Then the bathroom door closed. The toilet flushed. The sink turned on. Pammy did not come bolting out in silky underwear and thigh-highs. The door stayed closed.

Donna said, "Oh Mathew, where are you?" from the bedroom and it sounded like an opera singer, someone making fun of an opera singer.

Matt leaned into me and said, "You got a condom?"

I shook my head. I shrugged. I never had a condom. If I was with a girl and there was a condom involved, the girl had bought it, brought it, ripped open the package, and put it on my erection, while I monologued about how it was going to ruin everything. I looked at Matt again. He did not look good. I patted my front and back pockets like I could pound a condom into existence by slapping my jeans in a concerned way.

Matt pulled out his wallet. He flipped through the money. It was a big wallet but the folds, except for a few bills, were empty.

Matt, mumbling to himself, said, "Fuck me."

I didn't know what he was thinking. I mean, I knew what he was thinking: Susan, her belly, what was growing inside, the money we still didn't have; but I didn't know why he was thinking it now. If he was so worried about Susan, he should have been home with her, or he shouldn't have flagged down two middle-aged women who were into Miller beer and having sex with under-aged boys.

He whispered, "I don't need any more fucking babies."

I said, "Be careful," like the words were all the protection he would ever need.

I assumed Susan and her missed period was a fluke, and I assumed Matt took it to be a fluke, too. The pregnancy hadn't even been confirmed. Everything that had happened to Matt had either not happened or it could be undone for three hundred bucks. We were not, to my mind, in crisis mode. Or, if we were in crisis mode, it was outside, at school and home and when we were plotting to steal money from the paint store. Inside this apartment was the opposite of that. The opposite of crisis.

Donna, in a mock sexy voice, said, "Oh Mathew. Where are you my little rock n' roller?" Then she made a loud purring noise.

Again, I said, "Just be careful."

He said, "I was careful. Look where that got me."

I said, "Come on, dude."

He said, "Fine."

I said, "Okay."

He said, "Fuck me. I'm a retard," and headed for the bedroom.

I stood there with my beer. I loved bottled beer. Within the last fifteen minutes, I had fallen in love with apartments, especially ones with purple and green walls and fuzzy chairs. I loved Mick Jagger bobble-heads. I loved lingerie.

But as soon as Matt closed the door, I regretted everything. I moved towards Donna's bedroom. I put my ear to the door. I waited. I listened. I spun and tried my other ear, but I couldn't hear anything, not Matt making excuses or Donna doing her impression of a cat.

I turned and looked at the bathroom door. I thought about Pammy in there, maybe pulling up a stocking, or, for all I knew, washing her pussy. Maybe she was making things extra special, even sexier. I took two steps to Donna's door. I took two steps back.

I thought: Matt, babies, money.

I thought: I love beer and this apartment and middle-aged women in lingerie.

I walked into the living room and sat down on an old couch that had been re-upholstered with a lime green fuzzy cover. I finished the beer I'd been accidentally spilling and went for another. Miller was not a bad beer. I went back to the couch. The fuzzy green cover made everything feel like an expensive sweater. I leaned back and closed my eyes. Then I gave my dick and balls a squeeze to make sure everything was ready to go.

CHAPTER 7

Ten more minutes passed. Then twenty. The water was still running in the bathroom. I stared at the Janis Joplin clock in the kitchen. If something was going to happen, it needed to happen soon. This was a school night. I wasn't joking when I thought that. I had parents. I believed they were idiots but not enough to treat them like idiots.

Matt and Donna were making noises in the bedroom. I couldn't tell if they were fucking, but she was talking in a sexy voice, and he was sort of moaning. The bed was quiet, though, and nothing was smashing into the wall. This is stupid, I thought. Matt's Nova was only a block away and if I bailed, he wouldn't be stranded.

I turned on the TV and popped in the Rolling Stones concert. There was a homemade label on the box and someone had written "12/82 Tattoo You Tour Boston." The first song was "Start Me Up." The sound wasn't the best, but Mick was all over the stage. I went to the fridge for another beer, my fourth or fifth. I needed to leave. I wanted to stay. I felt a serious buzz coming on, and I knew another beer would make my decision.

Pammy came out of the bathroom. She was in panties and her tanktop. The panties were skimpy blue bikinis. Her legs, like her arms, were thin and muscular. The tanktop barely covered her flat belly. Her shoulders had dropped, and she looked tired. She had tan lines, and I could see that these weren't the panties she'd worn in the tanning bed. It was obvious she'd been crying, but she was smiling now, like something had been a misunderstanding and it had finally been worked out. If she would have asked me to leave, I would have left.

She said, "Hey," and sniffled.

I said, "Hey."

She said, "Rolling Stones?"

"Mick looks pretty good for an old man."

I didn't know why Pammy came out of the bathroom or even why she'd stayed in. She could have killed me or proposed marriage.

Pammy kneeled in front of me. It was sexy, but it was also tender. Tenderness made me uncomfortable. A woman in bikini panties I knew what to do with. A strange woman in her underwear, drying her tears, felt like retreat.

She said, "It's just that I'm new to all this."

"That's okay," I said, but I didn't know what she was new to.

She said, "You looked so nice and you were so fun and I hadn't been hit on in so long. My divorce isn't even through yet. I just... I don't know. Maybe I should start drinking more. That might help."

"I don't think we have enough beer for everyone," I said.

"See?" she said. "You make me laugh."

This was all a little deep, but I put my hand on her face, then, without even a hint of tact or kindness or sympathy, on her tit. I waited for her to pull away or stop. She didn't. I kissed her and started feeling her up. If she thought this—fingers and mouths—would make her feel better, I would have turned my whole body into hands and lips.

We kept kissing, moving our heads, changing angles. She tasted like toothpaste. I was sure I tasted like beer. I pulled her tanktop over her head. She stood up and pulled down her panties. Before I could get a good look, she was back down on her knees, undoing my belt. I got my hands in there and tried to make things faster. My hard-on popped out. She immediately started sucking and making noises like I was doing things to her, which I wasn't.

She stopped sucking. She looked at my cock. She said, "Oh god," like it was the best or worst thing she'd ever seen. She looked at me, looked at my cock again, and went back down. I moved to get more comfortable, and I could see her hand between her own legs.

"That feels good," I said, and I knew I was about to come and I tried to stop it.

I looked down at Pammy and the way her lips made me disappear. I closed my eyes and tried to imagine something else. I thought: please don't. Then I repeated it inside my head like a mantra: please don't come. I looked at the blackness behind my eyelids and thought hard about the blackness and tried to imagine a life without sex. The sounds of Pammy blowing me filled the room and my visions. Closing my eyes did not help. Pretending I was in the dark instead of being blown was not a defense.

She backed away and said, "Are you getting close to coming?"

I said, "A little bit."

Pammy said, "I know," and smiled. She said, "Do you want to fuck me? And just go real slow at first?"

I nodded my head. I did.

But I didn't, too.

I'd been whatever I wanted to be all night, and now I was going to come too fast and humiliate myself. It didn't matter how slow I fucked. It didn't matter if I fucked at all. My whole body was already there.

Then Pammy licked her fingers in a practical way that was still sexy. She went back to her clit. I licked her face. I didn't know I was going to do it until I did it, and then my tongue was on her cheek, then in her ear.

She said, "How do you want to do it?"

I said, "Trade me places."

She said, "Is that the way you want to do it?"

I said, "Yeah."

She said, "Just me on my back?"

I said, "Yeah."

She said, "Oh." She said, "Okay then."

I knew she was asking if I wanted to fuck her doggie style. I knew she was asking to get on her hands and knees and bend over the couch. I also knew that I couldn't take that. I couldn't have a fantasy, a vision really, of Pammy on her knees, bent over the couch, and then live out that fantasy minutes later.

She said, "You are so kind."

I said, "You are so hot."

She said, "You are, you're so kind."

She pressed her face to my face and held me. It was sexy and calming. I would have stayed there, rested, stayed on my knees, like a timeout during a football game where the players got air and re-focused, but she backed away.

She said, "Do you think I have pretty eyes?"

I said, "I do."

She said, "I think you have pretty eyes, too."

We finished switching places. I was on the floor. Pammy was on the couch with her hips hanging over the cushions. I pushed in, I pulled back, I pushed in. I knew I was going to come. I wanted to do anything but come. I knew coming was wrong, like a sin, like having sex before you're married. I was stupid. I was going to come and ruin everything. I'd waited for this, and now it was here, and now I was giving it back.

Unless I could come twice. Come, then keep going and come again. I had never tried it before, but I was so excited for Pammy as she lifted her own legs in the air, I believed that one orgasm probably wouldn't get me off. One orgasm wouldn't make a dent in my hard-on. I looked at Pammy, and she had those eyelashes and those delicate wrinkles, and her nipples were hard, and her bush was trimmed and framed by the white skin that had been covered during her last tanning session. None of this had to stop. I could last through the ending and find a new beginning. I could be born again.

So I came. I made sure that I didn't look like I was coming, then I did. It was my secret, my new technique, and I would go on until I didn't have to go anymore.

Pammy said, "That feels so good." She said, "I haven't done this in so long." She said, "You're not mad at me, are you?"

I said, "What?"

She said, "You're not made at me because I'm...because you're...because of our ages?" She reached for my chest and said, "I'm not exactly in high school."

"I'm not mad at you," I said, and I reached up and pulled her nipple.

She closed her eyes again and started to lift her hips and push into me. I tried to tell if I was going to lose my hard-on. I didn't think so. I didn't feel as horny, but I didn't feel not-horny, either. I didn't know what I felt, but my dick was hard enough to keep going inside Pammy as she moaned and moved her hand down below her bush and started to rub. Her moaning was getting louder and more frequent. There was a rhythm and drive to her voice and breathing.

The Rolling Stones played something slow in the background. I wished they'd hurry it up. All my senses were still on, but they were distracted. The purple walls didn't make as much sense. The green walls were off. The carpet on the floor hurt my knees. I looked at Pammy. She was there but not as loud as the music. She was a hologram. I could see her, but only at certain angles, and the vision was soft and fuzzy and not focused enough to really turn me on. She was fingering herself, and I was bored. I knew it was exciting. It just didn't feel exciting.

We went on together like that for a couple minutes, maybe more, and I thought I might be losing a little bit of my erection. I looked down, and it looked like a hard-on, but it didn't feel like anything. I was numb.

Seconds later, she started to come. She unconsciously slapped the side of her thigh with her right hand and clenched her eyes shut. I'd made girls come before, but not many, so it was always this moment where I believed in everything good in the world, especially me and my ability to make a girl come, except that this wasn't really that because Pammy was getting off on me, and I couldn't feel it.

She said, "I'm going to," and didn't use the word come, and I thought: well, at least I didn't completely fuck it up.

The rest of her orgasm sounded like someone punching the wall. It sounded like a chair being thrown and a boombox being smashed. It sounded like static and crumbling plaster, like a world being dismantled, until Pammy stopped coming and the sounds didn't, and we heard Matt and Donna in the other room, wrecking stuff.

Pammy said, "What is that?"

I was still inside her. Her hand was still on her pussy. Her legs were still resting on my shoulders and chest. We both looked towards the bedroom. It was quiet for a second. She reached down and felt my hard-on and her lips.

She said, "Did you come inside me?"

I said, "No," and tried to look like that was a preposterous question.

She said, "I'm soaked." She said, "I'm so wet."

She looked completely confused, and I couldn't tell if she knew I was lying, or if she'd be pissed, or if she was on the pill, or if any of this would even matter once I pulled out and walked away from this night.

Another smash came through the bedroom wall. Donna screamed something, but I couldn't hear the words.

I said, "I think we should get dressed."

Pammy said, "Yeah, really," and we had another smiling moment.

I pulled out, and my dick, barely hard, was covered in come. Pammy went for her panties and didn't seem to notice. I felt better. I stood and yanked up my underwear. I pulled on my khakis. I buckled my belt. I was a mess. My wet pecker immediately glued itself to my briefs.

The screaming continued. This time Matt was as loud as Donna. Their voices were on top of each other like boxers in a ring.

I said, "Do they always fuck like this?"

Pammy, pulling on her tanktop, said, "I don't know." Then, "Donna said Matt just turned eighteen and she was going to give him a birthday bang because he was finally old enough. I don't know what they're doing. It sounds scary."

I said, "Yeah really."

She said, "You can come over here and hold me."

I did that, and it felt good. It felt good to hold Pammy, it felt good to be held, it felt good that we didn't have too look at each other and make exaggerated faces that said everything was okay, and it felt good not to be crushing a boombox behind closed doors.

I thought about Matt's age, eighteen instead of seventeen, and how Pammy must have thought I was eighteen, too, and someone, either Matt or Donna, had lied.

Then Matt flew through the bedroom door. His jeans were on but unzipped. His belt was through half the loops. His shirt was in his hand. Donna came through the door like a cop car taking a bend in a high-speed chase. She was furious. She was fast. She was dressed in an ugly white bathrobe, the opposite of a nightie, and when she reached Matt, she threw a punch, punches. Matt moved, and the screaming started again.

She said, "You little teenage faggot."

He said, "Get away from me, you fucking whore."

Pammy looked at me and raised her eyebrows. I did the same. We looked at the other two, twenty or so years apart, completely different shapes, both barely dressed, and it was like bad TV or porn or both.

Donna said, "You don't leave a woman like that, you fucking faggot. I'm not some little high school girl."

Matt said, "You're a middle-aged slut."

She said, "Get back here and finish me off."

He said, "You're fucking crazy. I wouldn't touch you."

I said, "Friends." I said, "Friends, come on. What are we doing here?"

Donna, without looking at me, said, "Pammy, tell your little faggot to shut his pie-hole before I fill it with my fist."

Pammy said, "Take it easy, Mike Tyson."

Matt, appearing calm, or at least less violent and more dressed, said, "Yeah really, just take it easy." Then he added, "You fucking douchebag slutbucket."

Donna said, "What?" She said, "What did you say?"

Matt said, "Nothing."

He kept trying to get his belt on. He made two more loops. The belt was almost back around front near the buckle.

Donna said, "You homo." She said, "You filthy little no-account homo, did you just have the balls to call me a douchebag slutbucket?"

Donna looked completely stunned, as if all the previous violence had been pretend, as if combining one insult with another was the final indignity she could stand. Her forehead rumpled into four deep lines. She wiped away that face, and her eyebrows bowed down and touched. She fixed her robe, tightened the belt, and fluffed her hair. I thought she was done, angry still but composed. I looked at her legs, her calves, what was sticking out, the purple stockings.

She said, "Answer me. Did you just call me a douchebag slutbucket?"

Matt said, "I sure did, you big droopy-titted loser," as he attached his chain wallet to his belt and pulled his shirt over his head.

Donna came at Matt again, more pissed than before, and she threw random girl punches, hard and fast but not accurate. Matt was ready. He stepped aside and grabbed her hair and tossed her from the kitchen into the living room where she fell to the floor. She rolled once and got to her hands and knees, like a dog planning an attack. Pammy and I stepped away.

Donna said, "Oh, now you beat up women, too, faggotboy?"

Matt said, "Don't touch me anymore, skank. I'm sick enough already."

She leaned back so her ass sat on her heels. She didn't try to get up. I thought she would. I thought she would find something and stab Matt or shoot him or kill him with a bobble-head or a clock shaped like a guitar, or she would crawl back to the phone and dial the cops. I waited. We waited. Matt turned and spit in the sink. Pammy and I stayed together, a statue.

I leaned into Pammy and said, "I should go."

She said, "Probably," and kissed my ear. She said, "Thank you," and kissed me again, on the cheek, and I felt something wonderful, and it lasted until I made it to the kitchen door and saw the gash above Matt's eye.

CHAPTER 8

Eat N' Park was packed with factory workers, truck drivers, bikers, lots of bikers, and late-night bar people. The only women were waitresses. A huge man with a black eye, dressed in a flannel shirt with the sleeves cut off, stood in line at the buffet. He had a bowl of soup in one hand, an over-stacked plate in the other. He was staring at the bacon-and-eggs casserole. He needed a free hand. He needed somewhere to set his plate. I was behind him, waiting my turn. Matt was in the bathroom, checking the new cut above his eye. An old guy kept bumping my back with his plate and apologizing.

The man with the black eye said, "Shit," and started to walk away.

I said, "You want me to scoop?"

He said, "That would help," in a voice like he'd swallowed a bear.

I said, "Lean your plate down a little."

He leaned his plate down.

Most of his face was covered in black hair. Part of his beard was braided. I scooped for him. He nodded and walked away. I scooped for myself. I wasn't hungry. I was anxious. I'd never come inside a middle-aged woman and lied and sprinted away.

Matt was in the booth when I sat down. He held a napkin to his forehead, leaning on his hand with his elbow on the table like he was bored.

He said, "It's not bleeding, but it's a big cut. It's wide."

I said, "Let me see."

He said, "I should keep the pressure on."

The napkin was white. No blood was leaking through. Our waitress walked by and looked at Matt. She asked if we needed anything. I ordered a Coke. She took away my soup bowl. I started on the bacon-and-eggs casserole. It could have been hotter. They could have cooked the bacon.

Matt said, "Her pussy stank."

I said, "Our waitress?"

"No. Donna. Her pussy stank."

"It did not," I said.

"It did."

"That's it?"

He said, "Pretty much."

I said, "Her pussy stank so she clubbed you on the forehead until you bled?"

"Sort of," he said. "I don't know."

I said, "You should try the casserole. It's making me less nervous."

"What are you nervous about? You got laid."

The waitress walked by and said, "Boys, come on." She sighed like she was one of these bikers' mothers, and these bikers were innocent and not bikers. She said, "Some us don't want to hear that talk. Okay? Okay." She was fifty with wide hips and brown hair. Her orange uniform made her look like she'd escaped from a chain gang.

I said, "Sorry. My friend's retarded."

Matt said, "It's true. I'm retarded."

The waitress smiled and said, "Well, speak in quiet little retarded voices." Then she whispered, "Quit saying the p-word."

I raised my fork to acknowledge she was right. She acknowledged me back and walked off, a stack of dirty white plates in one hand, a check in the other.

Matt leaned across the table and spoke quietly. He said, "I choked. That's what fucking happened. I started thinking about Susan being pregnant, and I just fell apart. But I didn't want Donna to know I'd fallen apart, so I let her suck me, and shit—you heard the rest. She turned into Hulk Hogan. What was I going to do?"

I said, "Go down on her?"

"What part of stinky pussy didn't you understand?"

"I'm just saying."

He said, "I'm not making excuses. I'm saying she stank. It was like no shower for three days, overtime at the restaurant, the heat got in there and did bad things. I'm not judging. I'm saying on this night, she had a stinky pussy. Maybe other nights, her pussy smells like chocolate bars. This night, it stank. And thank god, or I probably would have bucked up and fucked her. But that stinky pussy was like a message from god. It was a burning bush."

"It pains me to hear that," I said.

"It pained me to smell it," he said.

The waitress walked by again. She said, "You're saying nice things, right?"

I said, "Absolutely. This casserole is delicious."

The waitress touched my head and kept going.

Matt said, "What are we doing here?"

My plate was clean, and I was hungry. The line at the buffet was packed: a person over every item, and a couple of guys waiting to get clean plates. The fluorescent lights made everything glow. A cook tumbled out of the kitchen with a clear plastic bucket filled with breakfast sausage. The line parted. I wondered if I could squeeze in and get more soup. I liked the soup. It was hot. It didn't have any taste, but it burned my mouth.

Matt said, "I'm not hungry." He said, "I was scared." He said, "You ever been hit in the head with a clock radio? It fucking hurts." He said, "Let's go."

I said, "I'm thinking about getting some more clam chowder."

He said, "Christ. Really?" He said, "Fuck it. I'll get a milkshake."

I said, "You could put it on top of your head to keep the swelling down," then I went to get in line for the soup and maybe some fried chicken.

CHAPTER 9

The guy with the cut-off sleeves, the guy I'd scooped casserole for, was at our table. He said his name, Joey, and that was it. I waved. I said my name. I looked at Matt. He didn't speak. Joey was more than six feet tall. He looked at us. His eyes were gray and black like two piles of ashes.

   I said, "Nice to meet you."
   Joey said, "How old are you two?"
   Matt said, "I don't know."
   I said, "Like seventeen."
   Joey scanned the room like he was checking for cops, like he was checking for witnesses. He was huge. His head was a tree stump. I pretended not to know we were dead, but I knew. I knew we'd offended him or the waitress, or the waitress had told him we were offensive or she'd said that we dropped the p-word and the c-word and were disrespectful and disobedient. Joey was the waitress' husband or boyfriend or uncle or brother or all of the above.

   I looked at him, and I hoped he would at least take me outside. He looked back. His arms were covered in tattoos. The one on his right forearm, the biggest one, was of the Ghost Rider. It was mostly flames, but I could see the skull and the motorcycle in there, and a wicked chain was spinning above the Ghost Rider's head like he was about to lasso the naked woman further up on Joey's bicep or the dice rolling on his neck. Joey bent down next to our table. I picked up my fork and started eating. The food on my plate was mostly brown.

   Joey said, "So I picked up you guys' bill."
   I waited for something else but that was it.

I said, "You didn't have to do that," with a mouthful of hash browns and sausage. I picked up the ketchup and pounded the bottom.

Joey stood and walked off. I poured on the ketchup. Matt raised his hands in a question. I shook my head: don't speak. That waitress stopped again and explained that Joey had just paid for our meal. He thought we were nice boys. I thanked her. I asked her to thank Joey for us.

Matt said, "Did I miss something?"

I said, "Yes."

He said, "I thought that dude was going to smash us."

I said, "I scooped for him."

Matt said, "I don't even know what that means. Is that some sort of gay sexual term?" Matt touched his forearm, then his bicep. He pushed up his sleeve until it was over his shoulder. He said, "You know what? We should get some cool fucking tattoos."

I said, "That guy's hand was bigger than my head."

I looked down, and the ketchup had covered the hash browns. If I got more hash browns from the buffet and slid those on top, things would still work. The potatoes and ketchup would balance out.

Matt said, "Did you see the motorcycle in flames?"

I said, "Ghost Rider," and got up from the booth.

Matt said, "Where are you going?"

I said, "To see if anyone needs my help."

CHAPTER 10

It was almost one in the morning when I made it home. I stood in the kitchen and waited. My mom was asleep. I took off my shoes and carried them down the hall. I paused every time the floor creaked. The floor barely creaked. I knew the loud spots, the boards that talked back.

Jesus, having dinner with his disciples, was framed on the wall. So was my brother in his baseball uniform, and me, seven years old, in a tiny brown suit and tie.

The TV was on in my mom's room. My mom was under the bedspread. The bedspread was covered with blue flowers. The whole room was blue, even the carpet. The walls were light blue with a dark blue border. The blue border was decorated with purple flowers. The lamps on the nightstands were blue, and the lampshades were white with more flowers circling the tops. It was all so feminine, like my dad didn't have a say in anything.

When my mom didn't budge, I stepped into my bedroom. I could hear the TV, the audience's laughter. It was David Letterman, whom my mom hated, whom she would have turned off if she'd been awake. I climbed into my bed and hid.

My mom said my name. I rolled over and moaned. I hadn't been to sleep yet. I was still in my clothes. The blanket was up around my neck, tight. My mom said my name again. I sat up and opened my eyes like I was scared, like I was confused. I kept the blanket up high, over my work clothes. It was dark. My mom wore an old robe. Her hair was in curlers. I flopped back down.

She said, "Danny, are you awake?"

I said, "Sleeping," like a sleeping person might answer.

She said, "When did you get home?"

I said, "Sleeping."

She said, "Danny," but not loud, not serious.

I said, "You're waking me up."

She said, "Did you get to study?"

I said, "I did."

She touched my head.

I opened my eyes.

I said, "The math is ridiculous."

She said, "We can talk in the morning."

She turned and walked out. I thought I knew exactly what she was thinking: he made it home; I must have fallen asleep; I am not a great mother; I am a good mother; my son is home; he is safe; he hates math but he's willing to work at it.

The hall light clicked off. In her room, she dropped the remote and found it. The volume accidentally went up. David Letterman shouted something. The TV went off. I needed to piss. I needed to brush my teeth. I knew I couldn't. My mom would lie awake now, thinking. I could hear her bed, the pillows. It was the same thing with the remote, the volume button that went up before she could find the power button to turn everything off. My mom always dropped something before she climbed under the covers. I knew her habits and the sounds her habits made. I knew she was sad that my dad was away on work. I knew I was two people, one real, one created, one drunk and happy to tell lies, the other sober and studying hard.

The heater turned on.

Our furnace was loud, and I was thankful for the noise.

CHAPTER 11

The alarm clock sounded like a football coach blowing his whistle in my ear. I slapped at the snooze button. I stood up. I stretched. I'd meant to take off my shoes, but I'd passed out, and now my feet ached. I undressed. I sat back down. My feet felt like balloons that were being pricked but refused to pop. The prickling was worse when I stood. Behind the shade, the sun was out, but barely. It was 6:03. The bus came at seven. I'd fallen asleep at two. I did the math. The math did not favor school.

My mom was in the main bathroom. I could hear the water. The bathroom was bright pink with black and burgundy tile. Everything was old, but well cared for. My mom wanted my dad to remodel, to update things. I stood outside the door. The door was open.

My mom said, "I thought I heard your alarm."

The curlers were out of her hair, but the curls were still loopy on her head. Her hair was dyed blonde, almost golden. She had a small towel tucked into her blouse so she wouldn't fleck her clothes with make-up. That was her word: fleck. She was pretty for her age. I could see that, but I didn't want to.

She said, "Well, good morning."

She went back to her make-up. I stood there in my white briefs, my nuts crusty from everything I'd done. I knew I looked sick because I felt sick, even if that sick was just exhaustion and the desire to stay home. I waited to see if she thought I had the flu.

She said, "I'll be out of here in three minutes."

I said, "Take your time. I'll use Dad's shower."

I didn't want to eat cereal, but eating cereal is what I did most mornings, so I found a box and a bowl and some milk. My mom had some sort of diet drink. She was always on a diet, even when she was eating whatever she wanted. She didn't look like she needed to lose weight, and she never lost any weight. I started eating my Honey Nut Cheerios.

My mom said, "Well?"

I said, "They're good."

She said, "Not the Cheerios. The studying. How did it go?"

"Okay," I said and tried to remember my lies.

She dumped her diet strawberry milk in the sink and said, "You lose weight because those things are undrinkable." She rinsed her glass and left it on the counter. She said, "Do you think you're ready?" She said, "What are the PSATs anyway? Your brother didn't have those. Did he? Maybe he should have."

I said, "The studying was fine. It was just some book." I took a mouthful of Cheerios and made loud crunching noises. I said, "I'm ready."

She said, "Really?"

I said, "Really."

She said, "Your brother's not doing so good."

I said, "I know."

My brother was a freshman at Slippery Rock University. He'd bombed his first semester. Now he was on probation. My father was furious. He'd pinned my brother to a wall at Christmas break and said, "Look!" then stopped himself before things escalated. My brother stayed on the wall. Then he locked himself in his bedroom. In the garage, my dad worked on the car, kicked tires, and tossed around tools.

None of this was shocking. My brother had always been a terrible student. My dad had always been angry. But this was college, and everyone's failures had prices. Tuition. Books. Fees for student activities and other things we didn't understand.

My mom loved my brother. If he hadn't ever done well in school, she said, it was because he was bored. My mom had been bored. She had barely graduated from high school. Her parents hadn't graduated from high school. Church was important. Failing Algebra was not. My mom believed her children to be geniuses, geniuses in ways that schools couldn't or wouldn't grade. I was very polite. My brother had illustrated a poem for my great uncle's sixtieth birthday. My mom thought a C was a fine grade. It was important to memorize John 3:16 from the Bible.

My dad did not think a C was a fine grade. He did want to pay for Cs or Ds or Fs which were the three grades on my brother's first college report card. Going to church was not an excuse for doing terrible in school.

My brother wanted to be an artist. He was artsy. He wanted to draw comic books for a living. He wanted someone else to write the words while he did the illustrations. He had a character he'd been working on, Track Failure, a former pole vaulter who quit the team to save the world. Track Failure wore a sweat suit and carried a twelve-foot fiberglass pole.

Even my mom knew you couldn't draw that and survive.

Suddenly people were talking about school in ways that were usually reserved for God, but it was late, and almost none of it made sense.

My mom said, "It's important to do well on these tests."

I said, "I know."

She said, "Are you in any clubs? Colleges look very highly on students who are involved in clubs and extracurricular activities."

I said, "Extracurricular activities—what?"

She said, "I've been reading."

I said, "I'm on student council."

She said, "What about football?"

I said, "I quit."

She said, "I know you quit."

I poured some more Cheerios into the remaining milk in my bowl. I thought I might puke. It was the way the Cheerios crumbled to wet dust in my mouth.

She said, "You might want to reconsider football."

I said, "I will," but I wasn't going to reconsider anything.

She said, "Your brother quit playing track, and he's not doing so well."

I said, "He needs to go to class and quit drawing cartoons."

She said, "Maybe."

I said, "Definitely."

She said, "Well, go to school and do good. If you have an art class, drop it and take something in science or math." She kissed me on the head and went to finish her make-up, even though her make-up looked perfect.

I drank some juice. That was the most anyone had ever talked to me about school, about education and my future, and I didn't like it. I put the juice back. I brushed my teeth and put on my coat. I wasn't sure if I still smelled like booze, so I yelled goodbye to my mom and stumbled out the front door.

CHAPTER 12

The Weeds was an old field that had been cleared for construction then abandoned. Things had grown back, but there were paths and clear spots. Trees were overgrown. Patches of berries tumbled out over the high grass. Motorbikes dug deep grooves in some of the paths, and puddles formed and bugs buzzed around the water. It was a place for bored teenagers and older stoners who still lived at home. The cops knew about it, but it was too hard to reach.

Instead of the bus stop, I headed there. My mom would finish her make-up and drive off to the remodeled church where she worked with poor kids who couldn't read even though they were old enough to be in school, and I would sneak back home.

Along the main path, a small square had been cleared out, and someone was trying to grow pot. The plants looked dismal, small and yellowish and surrounded by weeds. I kept going until the path opened up into a clearing. The ground was covered in moss. Pine needles leveled the rest of the weeds. Two other people leaned against separate trees. They didn't appear to know each other, but I recognized them both. One had a bookbag. The other one, a girl, had black leather saddlebags tossed over her shoulder.

The guy was named Shawn. He lived in Wendell. Wendell was worse than West Hempfield, where I lived. I didn't even know why. Shawn had on faded jeans and a zip-up sweatshirt. His hair was long and greasy. He might have been stoned. I waved and he waved back. We'd been on the same Pee Wee League baseball team, but that was years ago, and now we smiled and pretended not to know each other.

The other person was Lauren. She was out of school. Maybe twenty. She had a lot of tattoos, most of them green. She dressed like Shawn, jeans and a sweatshirt, but she was bigger, more solid. She was built to fight or ride motorcycles. I'd bought weed off her boyfriend once, and it had been scary, though now she cracked a smile and waved. She could have been stoned, too, or drunk, or just bored.

Shawn said, "I'm waiting for the berries."

I said, "The what?"

He said, "The berries. I come here stoned and eat berries. They're awesome."

Lauren laughed and said, "I thought you were talking in code. I didn't know what the hell the berries were."

I said, "No one's going where they should be going this morning?"

Lauren said, "Fight with my dad last night before I went out. I'm waiting for him to go to work so I can sneak in." She looked at her watch. "I haven't slept in thirty-two odd hours."

Shawn said, "I haven't slept in a week. Plus I have a Physics test."

I said, "Hungover."

Shawn said, "That's simple."

Lauren said, "Do I know you?"

A green dragon's head peeked out from her sweatshirt and flicked its tongue onto her wrist and hand. It was a sailor tattoo, not homemade, but close.

I said, "I bought weed off your boyfriend."

Lauren said, "He's not my boyfriend anymore."

Shawn said, "That's why I'm not taking my physics test."

I said, "Her boyfriend?"

She said, "The weed."

Shawn said, "It's always the weed."

I said, "What are you doing in Physics?"

Shawn pulled out a bag of pot. It was a small bag, knotted at the top, with a couple joints floating around with the shake. He said, "I just look stupid. When my brain is functioning, it's top of the line."

Lauren said, "Let's quit that then." She said, "The functioning. Not the weed."

Shawn said, "Physics can wait."

I said, "My brother's failing out of college. He wants to draw cartoons."

Shawn said, "Cartoons or comic books?"

Lauren said, "No one I know goes to college."

I said, "Comic books, I think."

Lauren said, "I was going to go to the community college, then I didn't."

I said, "I know a guy who failed out of the community college. He got a .25 grade point average. He got a D in gym or something, that's it."

Shawn said, "That's awesome."

Lauren said, "Not really."

I said, "I'm so tired," but when they passed me the joint, I got stoned.

CHAPTER 13

There was a knock on the front door. It was a gentle knock, like a person using only one knuckle. It went: plink. I was back in bed. I was under a big blanket and propped up with two pillows. The furnace was on. I was stoned.

I ignored the plinking. The plinking got louder. There was a thump. A thump was worse than a plink. I kicked off the blanket. Truant officer, I thought, though I didn't even know if such a person existed outside of the movies. My mom could have come home for lunch and not been able to find her keys. I sat up and listened for the next knock. Then, as a measure of extreme caution, I crawled under my own bed.

Being under the bed and being stoned were working against each other.

I looked up and saw my mattress. It was old. I'd had it since I could remember. A piss-stain shaped like a lake covered the striped fabric.

I heard my name. Then a knock on my bedroom window. I listened. I focused. It was not the truant officer or my mother. It was Matt. He was yelling as quietly as he could. I looked at the piss stain. I must have been six or seven the last time I'd wet the bed. Matt thumped his fist on the window, steadily punching the glass. I sat up and my face smashed into the wire mesh that supported the bed.

Outside the window, Matt stood in the middle of some rocks and shrubs that my dad had landscaped the summer before. Beyond the bushes, Susan had backed into the pine trees and stood there like a statue, like she was trying to make herself invisible.

She looked fatter than I remembered, puffed out, but not in the belly like she was pregnant, just in her face, like she'd gone crazy at Burger King. Matt saw me and waved.

I opened the window and said, "Dude, what are you doing?"

He said, "You weren't in school. I got worried."

I said, "No one is supposed to know I'm home."

He said, "Let us in."

I said, "Hi Susan."

She said, "Hi Dan," and waved a very sad wave.

I said, "The door by the garage is open." I said, "You could have called." I said, "You scared the shit out of me," but they were already heading down the driveway.

Matt took Susan by the hand. It was the same hand he'd used to toss Donna to the floor by her hair. There were so many stories. Matt's head was turned so I couldn't see his cut, if it was better or worse. I wondered what Susan knew. Lies had been told, I was sure, and lies needed to be told, and I didn't know what was expected of me.

I opened my bedroom door as they were coming down the hall. Susan had her shoes in her hand. Matt didn't. They both looked lost. Matt had combed his hair in a way that covered his gash. His usually out-of-control, rock-n-roll hair looked styled and moussed and ridiculous.

I looked at Susan and said, "You didn't have to take your shoes off."

Matt said, "I told her that."

Susan said, "My mom won't clean. She thinks it's degrading when women clean. We have a woman who cleans our house once a week. I have to leave my shoes by the door. I never know what to do at other peoples' houses."

"My mom's more into religion," I said. "She's not much for the vacuum cleaner."

Matt said, "Susan wants an abortion."

For a second, I thought they wanted me to perform the abortion in the bathroom or the basement, with a clothes hanger or pliers or my hands or something terrible.

Susan said, "I trust you. We trust you. Matt said you would know what to do." She started to cry and said, "I'm really really scared." She dropped her shoes and slowly put her arms around my neck. She put her face into my chest and started to bawl. The heat came off her like she had a fever and it went into me. I put my arms around her body.

Of course, I would know what to do. Matt trusted me. Susan trusted me. I was stoned. I was exhausted. I would make a plan.

Susan's sobs turned violent. She heaved and gasped. I hugged her as hard as I could. I lifted her off the ground. The weight of the pregnancy was there, even if the pregnancy was not. She said, "Thank you." She said, "I am so sorry." Her hands were strong. Her voice was not. Everything was going to be okay, I answered. She kissed my neck, my face. It was wet with tears and everything else. I held her around her back. I locked my hands like we were slow dancing. The harder I squeezed, the more stoned I felt. The more stoned I felt, the more intense my thoughts. If Susan would have asked me to put a gun in her doctor's face, I would have done it. I would have cocked the pistol and said, "You do not know this girl and you will not remember seeing her and you will never ever mention that she was pregnant." I would have pushed the gun barrel right up to his heart, right where he was used to pushing his stethoscope on other people.

But she didn't ask that. All she wanted was an abortion. I'd heard the words come out of her boyfriend's mouth.

I opened my eyes and realized Matt was part of our hug now. One arm was on my shoulder, the other clutched Susan's neck. It wasn't the same thing, the same touch, but he was there, part of it. I kissed Susan's head. I did the same to Matt. Down the hall, there was sun, and I could see the dust particles lined up like a tractor beam we could all step in to.

I said, "Okay, let's go in the living room. Let's everybody sit down and talk and try to make some sense out of this."

Susan said, "Okay." Then, while sniffling, "Where's your mom?" She said, "I snotted on you," and reached for my sweater.

I said, "It's okay," and laughed.

She said, "I'm going to cry again."

I said, "Don't." I said, "My mom's at work."

She said, "Okay. Okay." Then, "Your dad, too? Is he at work? I'm sorry I'm asking so many questions. Matt doesn't tell me anything."

Matt said, "How would I know where his dad is? I don't know where my own dad is."

Susan, "You should pay attention."

I said, "It's okay. My dad's out of town, getting some training or going to a seminar or something for his job."

She said, "We thought you'd be at school."

I said, "I usually am," and left it alone.

She said, "I guess we panicked. I panicked."

"We're done with that now," I said.

Susan bent down and picked up her shoes. The shoes were tiny, brown leather with silver buckles. She stood up and headed towards the living room. I looked at Matt's cut. He shook his head, meaning: don't worry. I was worried.

In the living room, I sat down in the Lazyboy rocker. Nobody ever sat there because the springs poked your ass and it squeaked when you rocked, but the loveseat looked too large for one person to fill and Matt and Susan were on the couch, like bookends, each resting on an arm, the middle cushion empty between them.

I said, "Okay." I said, "Well." I said, "Jesus." I said, "I'm glad you two came." I thought I should say something to Susan, but I didn't know what. The longer this went on, the more I lost my vocabulary. I said, "Okay." I said, "Who wants a drink? I feel like we should have a cup of tea or something."

Susan wiped at her eyes. She smiled. Her hand sort of jumped and she settled it with her other hand. I felt like that, like my body might pick its own direction.

Matt said, "I could sleep," and leaned back and closed his eyes.

Susan said, "Not now, Matt," and he sat back up.

Matt said, "Sorry to be tired," and huffed in a sarcastic way.

Susan said, "Stop."

I looked at Susan. She looked away, like everything that had happened, was happening, had taken away her right to look someone in the eye. She picked at the fabric of the couch.

I was right, though: she had gotten fat. Not terrifically fat, like girls get their freshman year in college, but pudgy, like she had stepped back to elementary school and demanded her baby fat back from whoever was using it now.

She put her head in her hands and mumbled something, then said, "No, I'm fine." She said, "I need a tissue, sorry," and stood.

I said, "The bathroom's right there."

Matt flipped her the finger. Susan didn't notice. She straightened her sweater. In the bathroom, she sounded her nose. She lifted the toilet seat and flushed.

I tried to picture my parents and their friends in living room, sipping coffee and eating dessert. It all looked so unimportant.

Susan came back and said, "I'm fine now. Thank you," and sat back down.

Matt said, "You said that. We know you're fine."

I said, "Alright. Drinks."

I stood up and went to the kitchen. I looked at Susan as I walked by. Her belly looked fine, no bigger than usual, not that I had ever paid it much attention, but her boobs looked blown up. Inflated. She had on a tight red sweater with some buttons down the front, and there was cleavage where there never had been cleavage before. But big boobs did not mean pregnancy. Big boobs could have easily meant candy bars, Pringles, M&Ms.

In the kitchen, I flipped on the light. I'd never made tea. I opened the fridge and grabbed a new 2 Liter of Coke. I made a mental note to replace it, so as to leave the house exactly as it was when my mom left in the morning. I grabbed three glasses from the cabinet and realized I'd need to wash those when we were done. I put the glasses back. I closed the cabinet door. The Coke went in the fridge, same spot, label facing out.

Back in the living room, I said, "Let's get the fuck out of here."

CHAPTER 14

Ten minutes later, we were at McDonalds in Irwin. We thought it might be suspicious, our eating when we should have been in school, so we hit the drive-thru. Matt had to rev his Nova to keep it from stalling out. All three of us were in the front seat, Susan on the hump. It was breakfast time, so we had Egg McMuffins and hashbrowns and Cokes. Matt paid. I offered him some money, but he waved me off.

Pulling away from the window, Matt said, "Should I park in the lot or drive?"

Susan said, "Drive." Then, "On top of everything else, I've never even skipped school in my life. This is the worst day ever." She said, "Sorry." She said, "I sound terrible."

Matt said, "I thought you'd skipped with me."

She said, "Must have been another girl."

I said, "I was probably the other girl."

Susan said, "I love Matt. I have always loved Matt. I'm sorry if I'm being mean. I'm being mean, I know."

I said, "You're not being mean."

Matt said, "She is. She's been like this all fucking morning."

"Let's all be happy now," I said.

Matt turned right onto Route 30.

He said, "Where to?"

I pointed up the hill, towards a strip mall. Shop N' Save, a local grocery store, would have a pregnancy test. A pregnancy test would provide answers. With food in my stomach, I was starting to think more clearly. Step one: make sure we have a problem.

Matt parked, and I climbed out of the car with my Egg McMuffin. The passenger side door to the Nova was a heavy wall of steel. A speaker had been built into the vinyl interior and the window was permanently sealed. I stood there, holding the door tight, and bent down to see Matt and Susan eating their sandwiches and drinking their Cokes. They looked like children, small angry children. Brother and sister. I loved them both.

Matt leaned towards me and said, "Don't get caught."

I said, "At what?"

He said, "Everything."

Susan wiped her mouth with a paper napkin and said, "Thank you. This is helping. The sandwich." She said, "You, too. You're helping. I'm sorry." She went back to her Coke.

I said, "Okay," and slammed the door.

Shop N' Save was an average grocery store. It was not as modern as Giant Eagle which had started to stock imported foods and fancy cheeses, but it was not as hillbilly as Peachins out in Hunker where the floorboards sometimes disappeared and your cart was suddenly rolling on hard-packed dirt and clay. I finished my McMuffin in Aisle 1 and ditched the wrapper in Aisle 2 behind a display for packets of gravy. A middle-aged man in a blue dress shirt and nice jeans looked up from the freezer he was stocking in Aisle 5 and said, "Can I help you?"

I said, "I'm just looking. Just sort of gearing up." That sounded stupid, so I added, "Just sort of thinking on what's healthy," which sounded even worse.

"Well," he said. "Gear up with this," and he handed me a coupon for a free pint of ice cream when I purchased a pint of equal or lesser value. He said, "Talk about healthy—there's a serving of milk in every scoop."

I said, "Thanks," and smiled politely as I moved on.

I tucked the coupon in my front pocket and made the next aisle. It was a good sign, I thought, that I looked old enough to be handed a coupon. Free ice cream surely meant that Susan was not with child. Or it meant the opposite of that. Coupons were for poor people who couldn't afford to pay full price. Free ice cream probably meant that Susan was with child. I took out the coupon and crushed it in my hand.

I didn't know where I could find a pregnancy test. I knew they were here, had glanced at them before, but not enough to recall where. Grocery stores were just starting to carry condoms, and there was still a good deal of shame involved with purchasing a Trojan, so I knew the pregnancy tests weren't going to be out front with the magazines.

I found an aisle with a sign that read FEMININE NEEDS, and checked there. There were douches and tampons and pads, but no pregnancy tests. There were diapers even, and baby bottles, but nothing to tell you if you'd need any of this stuff.

In Aisle 9, I found the toothpaste. Aisle 10 was hemorrhoid cream. We were getting closer, I decided. There were condoms. There was lube. There was, finally, a pregnancy test. There were lots of tests actually. I picked one up. I read the box. Pink was pregnant. Blue was not. I checked the price: twelve bucks. Twelve bucks was two cases of bad beer. It was five hours at the paint store, after taxes. I checked another box, and it was the same. Pink was pregnant. Blue was not. Twelve bucks.

I looked up like the glare from the cheap light bulbs was getting to me. I rubbed my eyes. It was wires up there, missing ceiling panels, dust. I'd been worried about two-way mirrors, but now I wasn't. I looked around fast and indiscriminately, like I wondered where my wife was and not like I was checking for an undercover security guard. I took two steps towards the front of the store and slid the thin box down the front of my pants. It was like I had an instant square cardboard hard-on. I kept walking and fought the urge to stretch my sweater down. I stopped at the magazine section by a closed cash register, read the headline on a tabloid, and shook my head like I couldn't believe how crazy those Hollywood movie stars were. I picked up the magazine, thinking maybe I should buy something, then decided a pack of gum would be more cost efficient and put the magazine back. I took my Dentyne to the express lane.

The express lane was empty. A middle-aged woman in jeans, a white Shop N' Save polo shirt, and a brown apron, said, "Anything else?"

I said, "That's it."

She had a friendly face, but she looked nervous and tired. Her eyes moved in too many directions. Her hair was dented in the back, like she'd slept in her car or dozed off in the break room. She had dangly earrings. Her fingers were red and glossy but chipped to pieces. It was hard getting old, I thought. Everything you do to stay beautiful just falls apart. She smiled again and raised her eyebrows. I thought she might be hitting on me.

She said, "Nothing else?"

I said, "That's all."

"Are you sure?"

"Just the gum."

"Nothing else?" she said and, I thought, looked at my crotch.

"I don't think so."

She shook her head up and down, exaggerated her voice, and said, "Nothing else you want to pay for before you walk outside?"

I said, "No."

She said, "Not forgetting anything?"

I said, "Nope."

She said, "Okay."

I said, "Fine."

She said, "Whatever."

I knew exactly what she was saying, but I didn't want it. I didn't want anything but to do what I wanted to do, which was steal a pregnancy test.

She said, "It's forty-nine cents for the gum if that's all you want to pay for."

I said, "What else would I pay for?"

She said, "Come on."

I handed her a dollar.

She said, "You look smarter than that," and handed me fifty-one cents.

CHAPTER 15

I was pretty fast for a big kid. When I was younger, coaches would put me at the big guy positions— offensive line in football, forward at basketball, shot-putter during track season—but I would eventually work my way to positions that required as much skill as strength: fullback, point guard, even pole vaulter where I could fly down the runway with the skinny guys then muscle my pole in a way they were never strong enough to do.

Even though I'd quit sports, I was still in good shape. My bench press was the best in my grade. I jogged. I skipped rope. I did push-ups until my arms went numb.

Thus, I believed it would be those two qualities (speed and strength) that would keep the undercover security guard from apprehending me.

Once I stepped away from the express lane, I spotted him by the exit, subtly blocking the electronic door. He was my height, but with stooped shoulders and a pot belly. He was at least forty, but he could have been fifty or sixty. It wasn't just age, but quality: he looked bad. His whole demeanor was slumped, so that even his face looked like it needed to sit down and rest. The mirrored shades he wore were trying to be cool but they screamed: narc! His shoes were dressy—not something good for sprints. Here was a man who believed that saying, "We need to see you in the backroom," was as powerful a method of crime enforcement as a gun, badge, and cuffs.

I was a good forty feet from the door when he made his move. He stuck out his arm like Dianna Ross in a Supremes TV clip, then he dropped the line:

"We need to see you in the backroom about some unpaid merchandise you're concealing."

That much I expected. What I didn't expect was the way he subtly moved a cart filled with groceries to block the exit.

My plan had simply been to bolt, to duck and run and be relentless. Maybe throw a shoulder. Hopefully not. If there were cops in the parking lot, I would zigzag and head for the woods. If the cops followed, I would outlast them. I knew my desire to escape greatly exceeded their desire to run me down.

But the grocery cart was a problem.

Before I could avoid the security guy, I'd need to have a clear escape route. The obvious thing to do was to start punching, but I didn't want to punch anyone, least of all a rent-a-cop, over a home-pregnancy test.

I was thirty feet away from the door. Then twenty. The security guard stepped behind the buggy. I took a couple huge steps, skips almost, to build up some speed, then launched into the cart like it was a linebacker trying to make ground on my team's tailback. I put both my palms into the front end of the cart and exploded. I followed through. I maintained contact. I did everything I'd been taught since midget football, and the buggy flew into the air, front end flipping over the back end where the push-bar and baby-seat were. Groceries went everywhere. The security guard, trying to get out of the way, stumbled and fell. His shades hit the dirty tile floor and slid like a puck on ice. Boxes of cereal and toilet paper fell around his head and chest.

I slipped down to one knee and skidded back up. I turned hard and rushed for the doors. My feet started to get away, but I hit the carpeted section by the gumball machines and made the front walk without going down. On the concrete, I picked up the pace.

There was the Nova. I sprinted for it then remembered I was being followed. Instead of climbing in the car, I ran past it, right down the middle section of the parking lot so Matt and Susan could see me and follow. They wouldn't be involved then. Nobody would get a license plate. They could pick me up down the road, out of sight somewhere, when I was out of breath, when the security guard had turned back to Shop N' Save and realized none of this was worth the twelve bucks I'd tucked away in my underwear.

I booked it past the diamond store. The used paperback bookstore was closed. I could run and read signs. The arcade was open. The movie theater had lowered prices to a buck. I took a hard right and bolted between the back alley and the daycare center. Barnes Lake Road was ahead and I slowed down. I stood in the weeds next to the birm and tried to breathe. I looked over my shoulder to make sure I wasn't being followed. I put my hands over my head. I'd just done the quarter mile, parking-lot style, in less than two minutes. I cleared my throat and hawked up a loogie. My lungs felt like they were being filled by a hair dryer.

A second later, Matt turned his Nova out of the parking lot and onto the road. I jumped from the weeds and waved frantically like I'd been stranded on an island for years and his blue junker was the first plane I'd seen in months. The Nova stopped. Matt revved the engine. Susan pushed hard to open the door and almost fell out. She rushed back to the hump. I jumped inside. Matt punched it and the wheels spun on the asphalt and you could hear the marks the tires were burning onto the pavement.

I said, "Drive discreetly."

He looked at me and laughed. He slowed down. Susan took a napkin from her lap and wiped the sweat from my forehead.

I said, "Everyone okay?"

Matt said, "What the fuck happened?" Then, "Should I be looking for a backroad or an alleyway or something?"

I said, "This is a backroad. They'd head towards Route 30 if they were looking for us."

Susan said, "Who's they?"

Matt said, "Yeah, really—who is they?"

I said, "The security guy."

Susan said, "What did you do in there?"

I was finally getting my wind. The breaths I was taking were cooling my lungs. My tongue wasn't as dry.

I said, "The first thing we need to do is find out if you're pregnant."

She said, "I thought Matt told you. I haven't had my period in a month."

"I know," I said. "But we need some official confirmation."

I leaned back on the bench seat, lifted my hips so my body was almost a straight line, and fished out the box that had been digging into my crotch.

I said, "Pregnancy test."

Matt said, "Nice work."

Susan said, "You stole this?" She said, "I have money."

Matt said, "Susan has money."

I said, "This was just easier."

Matt said, "Susan has money. She came up with two hundred and fifty dollars."

I said, "Where?"

Susan said, "My mom."

I said, "Your mom gave you money for an abortion?"

She said, "No. My mom has money hidden away. She's been squirreling it up for years. I don't know if she plans on leaving my dad or what, but she's got thousands of dollars up in the attic, buried beneath pictures in old shoeboxes. My mom thinks my dad is a pig."

I said, "Wow." I said, "That's good news." I said, "Easy enough, huh."

She said, "Yeah, I guess so." She said, "I've never stolen anything in my life. Not even a gumball. I just feel dirty."

I almost said: two hundred and fifty? I almost said: are you fucking insane?

Two hundred and fifty was not the right amount. Three hundred was not the right amount. Five hundred was the amount, maybe more. Two thousand was a good number. Three thousand was better. If you steal, and thousands are available, you take thousands.

But maybe Susan knew two hundred and fifty was the number. Maybe she'd sat down with a pencil and paper and a list of questions and a phone book, and she'd made calls and found the right answers. Maybe she'd called Family Planning and whispered into the phone while her mom walked around the house, not cleaning or doing chores or anything else that was degrading to women. Maybe Susan talked to a secretary and the secretary connected her to a nurse who handed the phone to a doctor. Maybe the doctor said, "Two hundred and fifty, that's correct."

If she had, I felt stupid. I was supposed to be in charge, I was supposed to be the hero, and the best I'd done was remember dialogue from an after-school special. Three hundred dollars for an abortion—what the fuck did I know?

I was fighting shopping carts and running from rent-a-cops, and Susan was in charge. She was scared, yes, and angry, and even mean, but obviously in control. She knew that crisis required thought first, then action. I had immediately assumed action was the answer, and we'd think later after we'd made our moves. I'd been wrong. I wasn't some sort of angel. I was an idiot.

Matt headed down Barnes Lake Road, staying the speed limit. He stopped at the stop signs. He didn't burn any more tire. Susan blew her nose. I took a sip off my Coke. The ice rattled in the paper cup. The road started to turn country. Trees started taking over houses. There were farms. Cows grazed in fields. I would have cranked down the window, but it was permanently jammed. I would have stuck my face in the breeze and licked at the fresh air.

I handed Susan the box containing the pregnancy test like I was handing over the rest of my life. In the box were my best friend, my robbery, two thousand dollars, and everything else I'd planned for the last month.

Susan read the box.

"God," she said. "Thank you." She said, "At least one of us knows what they're doing here.

Because I don't. If it wasn't for you, I'd be home, blubbering."

I said, "Really?"

She said, "God, I've been bawling for a month. It's all I do. I cry and I eat barbecue Fritos." She said, "Ask Matt." She said, "You just make so much sense."

I said, "It's not a big deal."

Matt said, "I owe you, bro."

I said, "You don't owe me anything."

Matt stuck out his hand, and I took it.

Susan said, "I'm just calmer. Not perfect. Just calm. I'm so glad you're here."

I reached down and cranked up the blower. My face was still sweaty from my escape. The fan filled the car, and Susan pushed into me with her shoulder, with her whole body, for a second before sitting back up straight.

Okay then. I was still captain. I'd been an idiot. Now I wasn't. Again.

I told Matt, "Turn this piece of shit around."

On a road the size of my bedroom, Matt managed to make a full U-turn with only one pull-up. He bumped into someone's shrub, barely missed a mailbox, and drove on.

He said, "So what the fuck happened in there?"

I said, "I tackled a grocery cart."

He said, "And?"

I said, "It rained groceries."

CHAPTER 16

Susan stood on the spillway. Matt and I sat at a picnic table that looked like it had been stabbed by an army of knives. There were initials on top of initials on top of initials. The only thing that was still legible was the word SUCK, followed by '81. The Nova was parked on the other side of the lake, in a parking lot that no one used anymore. I looked towards Susan. All I could see was her head. The spillway was dry and provided more privacy than any of the trees growing around Barnes Lake. She squatted down, peed on the test, and, I imagined, tried not to soak her underwear. I looked away as she stood and tried to pull up her jeans.

Matt said, "Back to the grocery store."

I said, "Some undercover bozo tried to grab me."

He said, "Did you hit him? Don't tell Susan if you did. She's acting cool, but I know she's freaking out inside. She's going crazy. And she hates violence. And she doesn't exactly share our sense of adventure."

I said, "She's not exactly acting cool."

He said, "Trust me, she is." He said, "And she only hates it when other people do violence. She's probably going to hit me soon."

I reached across the table and pushed his hair from his face to better see the cut above his eye. It was clean and only an inch long, but it was wide open.

I said, "What'd you tell Susan about that?"

He said, "We got in a fight with some Marines."

"Marines?"

"What was I gonna say? I got beat up by some bitch?"

"But Marines?"

"It sounded good at seven in the morning."

I said, "Should I know anything? In case she asks?"

He said, "She doesn't like to hear about that stuff. If she mentions it, just say it was crazy. They were tough, we were tougher."

Matt turned and looked towards the spillway. Susan waved. He waved back. She leaned against the concrete wall.

Matt said, "What's she doing?"

I said, "I don't know."

He turned to Susan and said, "What are you doing?"

She yelled back, "Waiting."

"For what?"

"The test."

"Do it over here," he said.

She said, "I'm afraid it will get messed up if I move it over there."

Matt looked at me.

I said, "I don't know. I don't think they're that sensitive."

He said, "Let's go over there."

I said, "Grab an end," and we picked up the table.

Even though the table had been whittled away, it was heavy. We lumbered along, dropping legs and pushing and picking it back up. Susan held up the pregnancy test. It looked like a fancy thermometer, something from a doctor's office.

She said, "Has it been ten minutes?"

Matt said, "I don't know. I wasn't timing."

She said, "I thought you had a watch."

He said, "I have a watch. You didn't tell me to time it."

She said, "I don't even own a watch. I had a Swatch like two years ago."

I said, "Wait five more minute so we can be sure."

Susan set the test on top of her purse which rested on the spillway. She was delicate with her movements, desperate not to mess up her fortune. With help from Matt, she climbed up the concrete wall and sat at the picnic table. Nobody talked. I watched the Timex on my wrist. Five minutes passed, but I didn't say anything. Surely, I thought, it was better to go too long than too short. Five more minutes passed.

"Maybe a minute more," Susan said, before I even spoke. Then she said, "I am so hungry. I'm starving all the time. I could go for a Big Mac. They're probably done serving breakfast by now, aren't they?"

Matt said, "I'm not hungry at all."

Susan said, "And fries."

I wanted everyone to be happy.

I said, "I'm not hungry, but fries sound good."

The three of us turned and looked at the test, resting on Susan's purse, resting on the spillway wall that separated the earth from the water, the water from the earth. Susan's face was so soft. Her body was so chubby and vulnerable. I tried to imagine her as the same girl I'd seen getting off on a Coke bottle, and it was barely there, the image, the feeling. I'd thought those pictures had said everything I'd ever need to know about Susan, and now they said so little.

Matt said, "I have to see the thing. I can't wait."

He jumped down and picked it up. He looked at the tester, moving it closer to his face, then farther away, then closer. He held it with one hand and moved his other hand through his long hair. The moussed style was going away, and he looked sane again, more like himself.

He said, "Which color is which?"

Susan said, "We want blue."

Matt said, "Blue is not pregnant?"

She said, "Blue is definitely not pregnant. I read the box three times."

He said, "You're sure it's blue?"

I said, "Come on, fuckhead."

Susan jumped up and said, "Give it to me."

Matt said, "I'm not being suspenseful. It's like green. It's like an ugly washed-out green-gray nothing color."

"Well," Susan said, taking it from Matt. "It's definitely not pink." She said, "Danny can you take a look?"

I jumped down into the spillway. Susan held the test like it was a million dollar bill and raised it to eye-level. I tried to read the line, but Matt was right: it was a gray-green nothing color. Of course, Susan was right, too: it was definitely not pink.

"This is good, right?" she said.

"It's not bad," I said.

"Should we celebrate?" Matt said, getting excited. Then, coming back down, he said, "Could it have gotten damaged? I mean, it was down your pants, and you were booking ass through the parking lot. Could something have gotten fucked up?"

"I don't think so," I said. I said, "Maybe." I said, "No." I said, "Fuck me. I should have taken two of those fuckers."

Susan said, "I don't know if we should cry tears of joy, or tears of..." and she stumbled. "Tears of whatever else," she said, and started to cry.

Matt moved to hug her.

She pushed him away.

He said, "Why do I even try?"

She said, "Why do you?" Then, "Just don't."

I pulled up a seat on the concrete and let my legs dangle. The concrete was cool. It was almost eleven, still early in the day. The sun was up, bright and yellow as a sunflower. I needed to be home by three or quarter after, just like I'd been at school all day. That gave us four hours. Family Planning in Latrobe was forty-five minutes away at the most. The office was downtown, maybe a mile from the airport. I'd been there with my old girlfriend. We'd gotten free condoms and foam. There was a big sign out front that said: We Do Not Perform Abortions. But I knew they did free pregnancy tests for teenagers and poor people, and I knew a pregnancy test in a doctor's office was better than a pregnancy test in the spillway behind Barnes Lake. There might even be time, if everything worked out, for Big Macs and Cokes and fries.

CHAPTER 17

Downtown Latrobe was a blip. There were brick buildings and, to a lesser extent, people. It was clean and boring. Every corner had a flower pot with purple flowers starting to bloom. The garbage cans, next to the flower pots, all advertised a different business. The businesses were mostly restaurants, and the restaurants mostly sold pizza. Years ago, when my dad had been working construction on the hospital, he said, "It's not a city. It's a borough," meaning there wasn't even a place to get a decent sandwich at lunch. Now we were lost. The town was a grid, every street clearly marked, and I still couldn't find the clinic.

Matt said, "What about Rolling Rock beer?"

Susan said, "Please."

Matt said, "I'm just saying." He started to point at something, what he thought was the Rolling Rock factory, and the front tire of the Nova slammed up against the curb. It was like a bumper car, and we were stuck. The rubber hitting the concrete made a peeling sound. Then we were on the sidewalk, my side lifted like we were about to be tipped. Matt oversteered to get us down, and the Nova dropped and bounced and swerved across the yellow line. I fell into Susan who bounced into Matt.

Matt said, "That wasn't Rolling Rock, I guess."

Susan said, "Jesus."

I said, "Wow."

Matt kept the Nova on the road. The three of us were smashed together like cans packed in a cooler. All of our arms braced against something, the roof, the dash, the steering wheel. My middle was against Susan's side, and it felt like I was humping her. Then I wanted to hump her. I wanted to wrap my legs around her and go. It was not an uncommon feeling, and it was not uncommon to have the feeling at the most inappropriate moments, but this shouldn't have been that, so I stopped it. Matt handled the road, and we all managed to get back in place.

Susan said, "Let's not get arrested. If possible."

I said, "You can't get arrested for hitting a curb unless a person's on it."

Matt said, "What about Rolling Rock though?"

Susan said, "What about it?"

Matt said, "It's a beer factory."

Susan said, "If we're going anywhere that's not the clinic, we're going to McDonalds or Kentucky Fried Chicken."

I said, "Swing back around towards the hospital."

Matt said, "I'm just saying. The Rolling Rock factory is around here."

Susan said, "Please don't wreck."

Matt said, "I don't even like the beer, but who wouldn't want to see a beer factory?"

Susan said, "You're damaged."

I said, "Turn right, then right again."

Matt said, "But I'll drink the beer."

Susan said, "What wouldn't you drink?"

I said, "I like Rolling Rock."

She said, "Danny, don't be Matt. I can barely stand Matt right now."

I said, "Let's not be nasty."

Susan said, "They're not going to put a beer factory downtown. They need water. Beer is made out of water. We're made out of water. Everything is made out of water. The whole world is made out of water. Get it? Do you see any water around here?"

Matt said, "There's these new things. They're called faucets. They pour water when you turn the handles."

I said, "I think she's talking about the babbling brook."

Susan said, "Exactly."

Matt said, "That's a shit creek. Everyone knows that. Just because they put it in a commercial doesn't mean they actually use the water. Maybe in 1929 or something, but not anymore. That's shit water. It's poison."

Susan sat one way. Matt sat another. They were as far apart as two people sitting on top of each other could be, their knees like arrows pointing towards different cities.

Matt said, "My dad toured the factory once."

"Good for you," Susan said.

Matt said, "Really?"

Susan said, "Good. For. You." Then, "Fuck. Head."

I looked at Matt and willed him to stay calm. He didn't. He lifted his leg like he was going to eat his knee then slammed it to the floor so the car locked up. Metal and rubber sounds came from underneath the Nova. The car jerked forward then rocked back then did it again with less intensity. Nobody had on seatbelts. I lunged towards the windshield and caught the dash. Susan slammed into the radio and air conditioning vents. The whole thing was like an instant storm. It hit and was gone, and everyone was thrown but Matt. He was steady. The car was instantly in park. Matt was furious. Susan was furious, not moving, but making a sound, a growl almost. I thought about the baby inside her, if there was a baby inside her, but I also thought about getting called a fuckhead and Kentucky Fried Chicken and Rolling Rock beer.

Matt said, "Say another fucking thing to me, and I drop you off, and I drive to Rolling Rock by myself, and you walk home."

Susan moved to the hump, holding her shoulder, less angry than I thought, more hurt. She said, "You do that."

I said, "Don't do that." I said, "And don't make any more sudden stops."

Matt looked at Susan and said, "Apologize. I'm not fucking kidding. You're in my car, with my friend, and I'm driving. Apologize. Now."

Susan said, "Fine. I apologize."

Matt said, "Fine. I won't kick you out."

Susan said, "I'm sorry I'm pregnant."

Matt said, "Great."

I hoped they were done.

They weren't.

Susan said, "You need a beer like I need this baby. How can you even talk about drinking on a day like this?"

Matt said, "You're a little girl. A tiny little dwarf child girl."

He held his fingers apart and squinted to show how small.

Susan said, "You're a drunk. You're a big drunk man. You're like my dad and your dad and everyone else. You weren't like this before."

Matt said, "I was thirteen before. Should I have stayed in 8th grade forever?"

She said, "Maybe."

He said, "Your dad's not a drunk. He's fucking lawyer. The guy's rich."

I loved the fighting, but I hated it too. Matt and Susan were terrible, but they were exciting and in love. If the world exploded, and it might, I wondered where I would end up, who I would end up with. Susan was so awful, she was wonderful. If she would have punched Matt, I would have punched him too. Then I would have punched Susan. Then I would have choked them both and kissed their faces.

A car came from the other direction. It was a blue car, but not like police blue. Two women were up front, the young one driving, the older one reaching over the seat to hand something to a couple kids in the back. They driver had a soda, the straw between her lips. Nobody looked at us, like we had made ourselves invisible.

Matt hit himself in the head. He did it again, harder. Susan turned but looked down. The Nova sat idling. I waited. I couldn't have said anything. The car engine slowed, then stalled. I looked outside at the buildings, at the sun. Everything had shut down.

CHAPTER 18

The clinic was not clearly marked like I remembered it, but it was there, and after more turns, we spotted the discreet sign. Maybe this wasn't even the same clinic. Maybe if you looked close, there were clinics everywhere, each one slightly different than the rest.

I'd been here—or somewhere like here—three years ago with my junior high girlfriend and her older sister. The sister, who acted like our mother, wanted us to be safe. She didn't think we should be having sex at our age, fourteen, but if we were going to have sex, we should not make babies. Making babies was the worst thing that could happen from having sex. She really liked us, was happy we were together, but she didn't approve. I didn't even know if I approved. I didn't know what we were approving of. I was not having sex. I wanted to, had tried to, but we were not. So I nodded from the backseat. When we parked, I noticed the big sister's nails: long and red. They were glamorous. It was like they'd been painted for sex. She put on her sunglasses. My girlfriend didn't have sunglasses. She looked small and confused. I felt small and confused, too, but mostly horny for the sister and her nails and her sunglasses. Then I didn't look at anyone or say anything. The girls went inside. Maybe I was supposed to go inside, too, but I didn't move, and they didn't wave me on.

When they came back, they each had a huge white plastic bag filled with condoms and foam and lube and brochures. I looked inside, and it was like a sex shop, what I imagined a sex shop to be like. I wondered how this stuff worked, if any of it was edible.

I looked at the sister and she said, "That smile is too big," and she reached back and wiped her hand across my mouth, but just joking, and I went back to reading the boxes and tubes in the white bag filled with sex.

The big sister got pregnant. Before that, their mom had found an empty bottle of foam in the garbage can and flipped out. My girlfriend kept giving me handjobs, and I kept touching her back, asking if it felt okay. We did not make a baby. Then, on the night when we were going to have sex, on the night she called and said, "I think I want to do it tonight," on the night we met in a field with a blanket and a towel, I put on a condom, and, before I could even lay across her, she started to cry, gently at first, then harder, then harder than I had ever seen a girl cry, and, for a second, I thought this might be rape, I thought I might have been raping her, whatever rape was. I took the condom off. I started to apologize. She said, "It's not you," and kept on crying. I wanted to cry too, to show I wasn't a rapist, to show I thought handjobs and touching were still okay, but I couldn't. My dick was hard and it hurt. We put our clothes on, then we wrapped ourselves up in the blanket. After that, we went home. I had three condoms, and I left them all in the woods, two unopened, one unrolled and empty. My girlfriend wasn't my girlfriend after that.

I didn't think of the Latrobe Clinic that night or any other night for what seemed like a very long time.

Matt said, "Is there like an emergency room?"
I said, "It's not a hospital."

Susan said, "I'm more nervous than I should be."

The building was a renovated Pizza Hut. Even though it had been painted, and the greens and reds were now beiges and browns, the old shape, the funky roof and the square bottom, was still obvious. We parked out back in a lot lined with meters. The meters lined up like an abandoned city made of silver towers.

Matt said, "How long do you think it'll take?"

None of us knew. We looked at the meters and I imagined time as silver change. We all checked our pockets for quarters. Nobody had anything.

Susan said, "It doesn't matter. I need to do this alone."

Matt said, "I'll come."

I said, "We'll all go."

Susan said, "That will look gross, like I'm a whore or something. Just stay. It doesn't matter. I need to do this alone."

Susan waited for me to move so she could climb from the car. I stepped outside. The parking lot was empty. There was a lamp post by the clinic and a sign hanging down that said: Government Funded. That sounded bad. Not so much the funding, but the government. Susan climbed out, then reached back for her purse. She straightened her sweater and hugged me and whispered something I didn't hear. She kissed my ear. Matt was in the car, down low. He couldn't see anything. My ear felt wet, tingly.

She said, "I don't even know which door I should use."

We turned and looked at the building. There were lots of windows, but only one door, single, glass, with a square handle, just like Pizza Hut.

Another car pulled into the lot. I heard the engine, but I didn't turn. Everything felt illegal, more illegal than smashing up a grocery store.

Susan said, "It's a fat old lady in a station wagon. I should go."

She went. I watched. Her shoulders fell forward. Her hips barely moved. It was the same way my dad walked down the driveway on Saturdays when he had to work overtime and he wanted to stay in bed.

I climbed back in the Nova.

Matt said, "Tell me I was right. Please. All she does is bitch at me."

"You're right," I said. "She's right, too. It's just a mess."

After that, we listened to Motley Crue's first album. It was a great first album, the kind of record that made you want to smash people's mailboxes with a baseball bat, and we both loved it, but it was not the soundtrack we needed. We were not drinking beer or huffing glue or running backroads at reckless speeds. We were parked. We were scared. I thought that, maybe, Matt should marry Susan. I thought I should be the best man, or maybe I should marry Susan. I kicked around some cassettes on the passenger side floor until I found Cat Stevens' Greatest Hits. I popped it in with the volume turned down. The acoustics guitars came on, slow strumming, and while Cat Stevens mostly sang about how awful the world was and how things never worked out between fathers and sons, he did it with bongos and lots of melody.

Matt said, "Better," and closed his eyes.

I said, "Much."

I don't want to say we were happy, but for a few minutes, we forgot to complain.

CHAPTER 19

Family Planning did not give us the answer we hoped for. They did not give us any answer at all. Thirty minutes later, Susan was back. She looked a certain way, professional but not, almost grown up but not, like how I looked walking from a job interview and wondering if the manager was serious when he said he'd call and realizing I'd chomped gum through all the questions. I turned up the Cat Stevens. Matt sat on his hands. At least I didn't do that. I climbed out. Susan looked at me and shook her head, but I didn't know what she meant. She climbed in the car, and I sat beside her and pulled the door shut.

She said, "The only reliable test is a blood test." Her sleeve was still up. There was a band-aid and, underneath that, a cotton ball.

I said, "Well?"

She said, "Exactly."

I said, "Exactly what?"

Matt said, "Yeah, exactly what?"

She said, "Drive first. I need to get away from here." She touched her face like it was putty, like she could get her cheeks to reform or stand firmer and with more confidence. She reached into her purse and pulled out a hot pink brush. She combed her hair straight back, which was not her style. She said, "Please not Cat Stevens," and hit eject.

They wanted to give Susan a reliable answer. "Reliable answers to important questions," she said, impersonating the nurse. "It's not a pregnancy. It's a potential pregnancy, and it should be referred to as such. Potential pregnancy. Unsafe sex. Not how many times, but frequency." She stopped her impersonation. She said, "What a bitch. It was like being in church. Awful. I thought it would be touchy-feely. I thought some mermaid would swim out and comb my hair and tell me I wasn't pregnant and good luck. She was like a nun. Maybe that was a Catholic clinic or something. I'm sick to my stomach."

Matt said, "But what's it mean?"

We drove past Kentucky Fried Chicken. We drove past the dollar movie theater with the ripped-up seats and the half-filled buckets of popcorn. The road was covered with potholes. One of the streetlights flashed yellow, but no one slowed down. We drove past the abandoned Dairy Queen with the sign that still said: Thank You.

Susan said, "No talk. Talking's not doing it."

Matt said, "I'm not talking."

She said, "Then don't."

I didn't talk. I had the window. I had the highway. Route 30 went all over America, from Philadelphia to somewhere in California. I liked beat-up towns and shopping malls that were going out of business because that's what I knew of the world, and it made me safe.

We drove past Arnold Palmer motors. The showroom was white brick and glass, an Arnold Palmer mural painted on the wall facing Route 30, Arnold raising his hand to say, "Hi," his hand in a white leather glove to better grip his golf club. I had always hated Arnold Palmer, but it had been fun to hate him before, and now it was not fun, not anything. Life had never been golf and new cars, but now golf and new cars looked like medicine we needed and couldn't have. Arnold Palmer had his own drink, an Arnold Palmer, one part iced tea, one part lemonade, sweet and expensive. It came in a clear glass bottle, and it cost more than a two liter of Coke, and I'd tasted it once, and it was wonderful, but I didn't know anywhere that sold Arnold Palmers and maybe I'd never tasted one, just imagined it, and everywhere else was fried food and discount movies, shutdown ice cream parlors and abortions you either could or couldn't have.

There was Latrobe high school.

The drive-in was up ahead, closed for years, the top part of the sign smashed out, the bottom part advertising a flea market.

Susan said, "It means my blood test will be back in a week. I have to call them." She said, "Then we can discuss all of our viable options."

I said, "What's to discuss?"

She said, "Our options? Like it has anything to do with that fucking bitch." She threw her head back and swallowed a scream. Veins bulged in her neck and subsided.

Matt said, "Jesus." He steered the car off the road, slowly, with control. We bounced along the birm. Then he took both hands off the wheel and covered his face. I reached across Susan and took the wheel. It wasn't easy to steer, but I did it until we stopped. Matt said, "Okay." He pushed the accelerator, but barely, so we did five miles an hour as we headed towards the drive-in.

A barrier had been erected with wooden horses to keep people out, but it had been hit and wasn't blocking anything. Ticket booths, all three, were destroyed. The bricks were in place, but the windows were gone, and the roofs all had holes kicked through the shingles. An empty keg, still tapped, sat upright on a door that had been ripped off and turned into a table.

Susan said, "I used to come here with my dad."

The screen was huge, but a giant tear scarred up the middle. Most of the sound boxes had been ripped out or kicked over. Beer cans and bottles were everywhere like someone had confused them with seed. There was more glass and tin than grass. Long ruts from dirt bikes cut across the main road. We bounced along. A bottle popped underneath us. Then another. Then it was the constant sound of glass breaking and cans being crushed. I didn't know how to change a tire. I didn't care about tires. I didn't know why they didn't fix the screen, and start the projector, and show movies when it finally went back to dark.

CHAPTER 20

McDonalds was packed, and besides, we'd eaten it for breakfast. I wanted to go to a diner. Susan wanted Burger King. She looked like she needed it more. The parking lot was being paved so we parked across the street at Taco Bell. The construction workers, the pavers and the guys rolling the machines, all stopped to stare at Susan. I pretended like they weren't. The smell was thick and black as the tar they were spreading.

We stood in front of the menu. No one was in line. It was the same menu we'd been staring at since we were kids. We kept staring. The dining area was empty. A man in a truck pulled up to the drive-thru. I ordered two cheeseburgers, ketchup only. Susan ordered a Whopper with extra cheese, fries, a Coke, and a large chocolate shake. Then, while Matt made up his mind, she added a cherry pie.

The woman working the register was old, maybe seventy. Her hair was blue and permed, and it poked from her Burger King visor in odd ways. The whites of her eyes were as gray as an old motel sheet. Her lips were as white as her cheeks. Her wrinkles had wrinkles, and those wrinkles were covered in age spots and raised by thick blue veins. Yet the polyester uniform made her look like a child swimming in adult clothes.

Matt said, "I'm not even hungry," then ordered a Kids Meal. He said, "The nuggets. With the spicy mustard."

The cashier said, "Kids Meals are for kids twelve and under."

Matt said, "Great. I'm nine." He looked at me. "Tell her, Dad."

I couldn't.

The cashier said, "We have toddlers toys for children three and under."

Matt said, "Just give me the Kids Meal." He said, "I'm not doing anything to you."

The cashier fixed her visor. She said, "No."

I said, "Just give him the six piece nuggets, a small fry, and a small Coke."

Matt said, "And the spicy mustard."

The cashier said, "Spicy mustard is McDonalds."

Susan started to cry. She put her face in her hands. She said, "Oh god." She said, "God, seriously, god." Then she quit crying and wiped away the tears. She said, "Okay. Okay." She said, "Fine, I'm fine." By fine she meant furious. She turned at Matt and screamed. It was short, a guttural bark, half a second, maybe less. Her face jumped off her head which pulled away from her neck. There were veins and a spray of spit. Matt flinched. Susan went back. She said, "Sorry." She touched her hair. She said, "I'm not sorry. I don't know why I said sorry." I stepped away so they could hit each other if they wanted to hit each other. Susan did it again. It was a ferocious sound, from a place I'd never been. She said, "Okay now." She said, "Well." She turned and ran for the restroom. I looked at the grease spots on the floor. I looked at her feet.

Matt turned and said, "I wanted the toy." He lifted his hands. He looked at the cashier and said, "I just wanted the toy. I wanted it to be funny."

The cashier pushed some buttons on the register and said, "You're too old for a toy. I said that already. Toys are for kids. They're called Kids Meals." Her eyes were there. Her lips, when they moved, were pink with color.

Matt walked towards the restroom.

The cashier said, "That leaves you."

I took at my wallet. I handed her some bills.

CHAPTER 21

Our school day, miles away from school, was over. We needed to be home. The ride to Youngwood, the east side where Susan lived, was quiet. Nobody fought or barked or locked up the brakes. Susan had another large order of fries and ate those, one at a time, taking two or three bites from each fry. I tried not to look at my watch. Matt turned on the radio. The radio was risky. Everything, except breathing and looking away, was risky. There was that sound in Susan, and I didn't need to hear it again.

The bus stop was near Park N' Pool and some old townhouses that had been painted institutional yellow and lime green. The bus hadn't arrived.

Susan kept at her French fries. She said, "I like this song."

Matt said, "Me, too."

It wasn't even a song. It was a commercial.

Susan said, "Is your band practicing tonight?"

Matt said, "I can't be in a band right now."

Susan said, "Did you tell anyone that?"

"No."

"You didn't tell your band that you're not in the band right now."

"I guess," Matt said.

Susan ate a French fry. Matt rubbed at the steering wheel like he was giving it an Indian burn. Bands were stupid. I hadn't known that before, but now I did.

I said, "Let's just all ride to my house, then you two can ride back together."

Susan said, "It's okay. There's a little park down the road. I'll go and sit on the swings. I need to be alone anyway." Then, "And you guys are sick of me."

I said, "We're not sick of you."

Susan said, "Matt is."

Matt said, "I'm not."

She said, "You should be."

Matt was as mangled as my parents' Cutlass the night I drove it into a tree. His eyes, like the windshield, were cracked.

Even his t-shirt was a mess, stretched out in odd places like he'd tried to adjust the fabric and failed. The sweat stains around his armpits were taking over. Now was a good time to leave. He couldn't leave. He reached down and tugged at his shirt. He itched his knee.

Susan was the opposite. She was a map that had been ripped apart then taped back together. The edges overlapped, but the pieces were at least in place.

I said, "Let's go see that little park."

Matt checked his mirrors and drove. He held Susan's hand. He kissed her wrist. She took it back. He adjusted the radio and steered.

The trees were blooming. White flowers tipped every branch. A few of the blossoms had fallen to the grass. The playground looked newly painted. The monkey bars were dark blue. The slide was orange. The frame of the swingset was red and white, stripes on a candy cane.

Susan handed me the French fry box. I thanked her. She crumpled a beige paper napkin into a ball and held it in her hand. I looked down at the box. The fries were gone. Matt reached for the air conditioner and the fan came on. There was shade a few feet away, but Matt never parked the Nova under anything, especially a tree, because of the paintjob. I held up the fry box to shield my eyes.

Susan said, "I'm afraid to have this money."

I said, "What money?"

Matt said, "The two hundred and fifty dollars."

I said, "Oh." I said, "Oh, okay," but I still didn't remember.

Then I did: the cash in the attic that her mother had been hoarding. Susan, the thief. Susan, with the prices. Susan, with the plan. It was good not to have to rob the paint store, even if I still wanted to rob the paint store.

I said, "You have that money on you?"

She said, "Yeah."

Matt said, "Just don't lose it."

I knew this other girl, and she hid her weed in the tip of an old roller skate.

Susan said, "I feel like it's trying to get out." She clutched her purse like it needed to be held down, like the money was a small rodent.

Matt said, "Just be careful. Keep your purse with you."

She said, "But I can't."

Matt said, "I'll keep it. I don't care."

I said, "He's great with stolen goods."

She said, "Don't make me feel any more guilty," but she looked relieved. She undid the straps so she could see inside. "You guys are being so good about everything. I keep flipping out. I'm the one who's insane."

I said, "No one's insane. No one's flipping out."

She said, "Come on, did you hear me in the bathroom at Burger King?"

I said, "Maybe a little."

Matt said, "I shouldn't have ordered the Kids Meal. That was retarded."

She said, "You guys are great. Both of you."

She pulled out the money. Then she pulled out some more. An envelope would have been better. Even a rubber band. She reached in, and the money came out in clumps, mixed between dirty tissues and hair clips. She piled the money in Matt's lap. Lots of the bills were singles and fives. The pile shifted and fell to the floor.

Matt said, "Slow down. I'm losing some."

She said, "God, that looks like a lot more than it is."

"But it's not?" I said.

"No," she said. "Two hundred and fifty dollars, to the dime."

"To the dime," I said, and I hoped she didn't mean silver change.

CHAPTER 22

My mom had been home and gone back out. A note explained everything. It was work. It was working with poor people. It was how poor people sometimes treated their children. She scribbled a big heart and wrote, "Be home around seven-ish."

Turkey nuggets were under plastic in the fridge. All I had to do was fire up the microwave. If I wanted a side, there was mac-and-cheese or instant mashed potatoes in single serving cups. I checked the nuggets. I lifted the plastic. The smell was like dog food. There were pieces in there, gizzards and beaks. I put the nuggets back and closed the refrigerator.

I opened my wallet and counted what I knew was in there. I went to my bedroom and pulled a twenty from my stash. I shouldn't have been hungry, but I was, and not for reheated turkey nuggets shaped like throwing stars. I called the Pizza Factory and ordered a large pizza, half plain, half pepperoni, just the way my mom liked it.

When my mom came home, it was almost seven. She looked exhausted. Her hair was flattened on one side like she'd been leaning on her hand for hours. She took off her rings and set them on the counter. She cracked her knuckles, which was against her own rules.

I said, "That bad."

She said, "Probably not."

One of her kids, her students, one of her six-year-olds who could barely read, had shown up to school with bruises on his back and the backs of his legs. It happened like that sometimes, and there was always extra work at odd hours, and the cops were always involved. It had gotten so common that my mom seldom spoke of it, or if she spoke of it, she didn't complain.

She said, "I don't understand people."

I said, "I know."

I thought she might have more, but she didn't. She leaned into the corner of the wall and scratched her own back by shimmying her shoulders. She closed her eyes. I was at the dining room table, a bunch of books spread out like I'd been doing something I should be doing.

I said, "You want me to scratch that?"

She said, "No." She said, "Yes." She said, "I'll just get it in the bathtub with my brush." Then, after a pause, she said, "These people don't talk. They fight. The husbands hit the wives. The wives beat the kids. The husbands and wives were all beaten up when they were little. The kids will grow up and beat their kids or go to jail or just die. It's endless."

I said, "They're hillbillies. They live in shacks."

It was true. We were talking about Smithton, the northernmost tip of southern Appalachia. The adults were illiterate. The kids sometimes ate off the floor. My mom had stories. She'd taken me to work. People had TVs but not cable. I saw a goat with its own house.

She said, "I don't care where they live or why they do it, I just want it to stop. You can be poor and nice. You can be poor and miserable and still not beat your kid behind the legs with a leather cowboy boot."

I said, "Remember when you used to hit me with a boot when I was little?"

She said, "Please. If I slapped your butt with my bare hand, you cried like a big baby." She stopped scratching her back and laughed. She said, "I feel like sometimes people should just watch us, our family. They could learn from us. They could learn things, then teach it in a class. At least we talk."

I nodded and looked at my books. When I looked back, she was scratching against the corner of the wall again.

This was the most I'd talked to my mother in months, maybe a year, and it wasn't a real conversation, just an aside about a family who was not us on an exhausting day.

I only listened because I wanted to skip school tomorrow.

Otherwise, I would have locked my bedroom door, and my mom would have eaten her turkey nuggets, alone at the breakfast nook.

If we kept going, if we talked again tomorrow or the next day, it would be shouts and accusations, my mom yelling, "I love you, but I can't stand you!" or, "Don't speak!" or, "Stop breathing!" then I would throw things around my room and bust my lamp and my stereo and my few remaining records. She would hide in the bathroom. The quiet that ensued would take weeks to become conversation then, without warning, noise.

I said, "There's pizza on the counter. Half plain, half pepperoni."

She took off her blazer and hung it on the back of my chair. It smelled like perfume and, from the cops, smoke. She opened the pizza box.

I said, "What do you think?"

She said, "Looks like heaven." She pulled out a piece and lifted it in the air like it was something to behold then lowered it to her mouth and bit off the tip. With a mouthful of cheese, she said, "You are a good son."

It wasn't true, but I believed it.

Which is why I was able to say, later, "I have a test tomorrow, and I've been studying all night, and I'm not even close to being prepared—"

And before I finished, she put down the brush she'd been running through her wet hair and said, "That's fine, stay home, you haven't missed in a while."

CHAPTER 23

Matt pulled into the Dandy Dollar parking lot. It was early morning. The Dandy Dollar was a grocery store near my bus stop. They sold day-old bread and pork chops and generic soda. I'd been behind a green dumpster, waiting for my bus to come and go, waiting for Matt to arrive. I was done with school. I knew I'd go back, but I didn't know when.

The Nova rumbled to a stop. Matt tapped the horn. I popped out from behind the dumpster. I hit a couple muscle-man poses: the double bicep then the crab. I hopped in the Nova. It smelled like cold French fries. The floor was littered with fast food wrappers. I stepped on a wax-paper cup. Soda and melted-iced leaked onto the mat.

Matt said, "That's Susan. We went for more fast food."

"When?"

"After I dropped you off, I went back to the playground, and she was hungry. You might have noticed that she's been hungry."

I said, "I might have noticed."

He said, "Let's get out of here." He said, "I'm so glad we're doing this. I couldn't face school today." He extended his arms and pushed up like he was trying to make a convertible out of a hard-top.

I said, "Let's roll."

Matt said, "I'm still celebrating," and he matched my muscle-man poses. He revved the Nova a couple times and the engine sounded like a hurricane.

Matt looked less tense, more fun. The gash on his forehead had scabbed over in an ugly way but at least he wasn't trying to hide it with a feather of hair. Around his neck was a silver chain with a tiny medallion that said Satan in Latin, or what the evil hippy selling the medallion had translated as Satan. Matt had on his KISS Destroyer t-shirt.

I had on jeans and the Poison t-shirt I'd bought a concert last summer. At the show, I'd drunk twelve beers and thrown up in the trough in the men's restroom. Susan had been at the show with a couple friends, but not Matt who was roofing houses with his dad. I saw her in the parking lot before the music started, but she wasn't drinking, and I was worried I wouldn't have enough time to finish all my beers. I said, "Hey," and stayed focused on the cans in the cooler. She said, "Beer, huh?" and I said, "Yeah."

Now she was home, in bed, playing hooky, still not drinking.

Matt said, "I'm glad Susan's home. I couldn't take her again."

"She's stressed," I said.

He said, "This is a good idea, man."

I said, "Truancy always is."

He said, "Where do you learn a word like truancy?"

I said, "You know truancy."

He said, "I know truancy, but I would never use truancy."

I said, "Drive somewhere."

He said, "I'm thinking."

I said, "Think faster."

If yesterday had been our mistake, today was our do-over. Matt had on cologne, Chaps by Ralph Lauren. I was wearing the same thing. Chaps came in a bottle that curved like saddle. You could get a lot accomplished when you smelled like a cowboy.

Matt said, "Let's do something good today."

I said, "Let's do something great."

He held up a tape. I took the cassette and popped it in. The sun was a blazing. There were clouds, but they were white and far apart. I put on my seatbelt. Matt found reverse. The music was loud but mellow. It was a mix-tape, mostly ballads but by heavy metal artists. All the songs said the same thing: it's okay to take a three-minute break from fighting and fucking and drinking; love your girlfriend and be sad; unclench your fist and hold someone until it's time to rock again.

Matt said, "Where to?"

I said, "I don't know."

I meant it. I didn't know. Part of my brain was starting to shut down. I knew enough to be sad and worried, but I liked being happy instead. I liked the sun and the music more than I liked abortions and pregnancy tests. I told Matt to turn left on Wendell Road, away from school and home, out into nowhere.

CHAPTER 24

I said, "We should get some beer."

Matt said, "I thought we were going to do something great today."

I said, "Beer's great."

He looked like he wasn't sure. He pushed his bangs back and held them there. He touched the scab above his eye. The scab looked ready to drip brown blood or something yellow.

I said, "We could have a great day." I said, "Or not, you pussy."

He said, "I didn't say I was against having a great day."

I said, "Drive to Herminie."

He said, "Where the fuck is Herminie?"

"Two more miles thataway," I said.

Matt blew through a stop sign and headed south.

He said, "Why have I never heard of Herminie?"

"Mot of the kids who live there go to Yough," I said. "But Sam lives there."

Matt said, "Sam, yeah."

Samantha Bonmarito had been my junior high sweetheart. She was a year older than me, and we stayed together while she was in high school and I was in junior high but when I came to high school, that was it. We broke up because teenagers break up, but it was sad and ugly. I called her names. She slept with a football player from Notre Dame on a weekend visit. I sent her a note that said, "Dear Sam, you are a whore." She slapped me at a bonfire in front of six hundred high school football fans. She tried to run me over with her Honda. I jumped and launched a large cherry Slurpee at her windshield. Now, when we saw each other at school, we looked the other way or pretended to be overly happy to be talking to someone who was not our beautiful first love.

Matt said, "Sam. God, she was built to screw."

Sam didn't know anything about sex, and it took me months to get her clothes off, and we talked a lot about being together forever, and then, suddenly, she knew everything about sex. She took what I did, then what we did, and turned it into all the things we'd heard about in school or the neighborhood and seen in movies and into things we hadn't heard about in school or the neighborhood and seen in movies, too. Late nights, she would show up at my bedroom window with a blanket and a can of Lysol and we would sneak into my neighbor's yard and fuck in a doghouse that had been abandoned by a huge Doberman Pinscher. "Dog germs," Sam would say before spraying everything with Lysol and unfolding the blanket.

Sam had never gotten pregnant. Her period came when it came, and it was more of a disappointment than a relief. It was not easy to have sex on her period in a doghouse. Every month we started again and worried less than the previous month. Instead of feeling lucky or grateful or blessed, I felt untouchable. It was not like Lucy Arms, my chubby neighbor. It was not like any of the girls I'd slept with before. Sam was bulletproof against pregnancy. I was the superhero of not getting girls knocked up. I sometimes wondered if the weed and the beer had done something to my sperm, had killed the cells that made the babies. I hoped it had.

Matt said, "You ever fuck Sam with rubbers?"

I said, "Sure." I said, "Sometimes." I said, "Twice, I think. The first time and maybe one other time. The other time it broke."

He said, "You pull out?"

"Mostly."

"Was she ever late?"

I said, "She never kept track of her period."

He said, "You're a lucky fuck."

"I know," I said, but it was a gift, not luck.

CHAPTER 25

Tillbrook Road was mostly farms. In the summer, there were fields of corn and cows and miles of weeds that hadn't been plowed or planted. Now, in the spring, it was mud and grass. Corn stalks, a few standing, most of them knocked to a few inches off the ground, dotted the scenery. There was one barn, an old gray thing, and a farm house from the previous century that the owners kept immaculate. The silos in the distance were half-filled or less, and the cobs were almost colorless after the winter snows and the early spring rains. The creek that ran along the edge of the road was high and fast, and I imagined we could get a raft in there and go or just fish or go under or not go anywhere at all.

Matt said, "What'd you say about beer?" He said, "The more I think about it, the more I think being drunk might be the answer."

I said, "I would like to not go back to school."

He said, "I'm working on it."

I said, "Ever." I said, "I would like to not go back to school, ever."

"I'm working on it."

"How does someone work on that?"

Matt said, "I borrowed this press, this silk-screen thing my dad uses at the office. You can do everything with it—make t-shirts, signs, whatever—but you can also do paper stuff. You can do those, like those little tablets—what are those called?"

I said, "Stationery," and I knew what he meant: a doctor's excuse.

He said, "So we get some stationery, and we write like Joe Blow Doctor at 101 Doctor Street or wherever, and who's gonna question that?"

"One problem," I said.

"Yeah?"

"Phone numbers. Those things always have phone numbers."

"No one calls those."

"They might."

"Why?" he said.

"If we start missing a lot of days, someone's going to call someone."

Matt said, "How's your grades?"

I said, "Unbelievably average."

"How average?"

"Bs and Cs and a couple As mixed in."

"That's not average," he said.

I said, "Last year, it was mostly As."

"I'm looking at Cs and Ds, and like an F or an F+ maybe."

I said, "That's not average. That's a little retarded." I said, "If you go missing, no one will care." I said, "They might be happy."

Around the next bend, Shawn, the stoner who'd been avoiding Physics, the kid I'd smoked pot with in The Weeds only yesterday morning, ducked behind a small bush and crawled from that bush to a Weeping Willow with branches that reached the ground.

I said, "Slow down. I know that kid."

Matt said, "That's not a kid. That's a Vietnam veteran."

Shawn was dressed in camo. It looked like he was carrying a small shovel.

The Nova stopped and I opened my door. I said Shawn's name, then my own. He crawled deeper into the Weeping Willow. I called his name again. Flat on his belly, he poked his head out and adjusted his glasses.

I said, "You okay?"

He said, "I'm growing weed."

I said, "What?" I said, "Where?"

He said, "Incognito." He made a motion with his hand, flat and extended, cutting through the air. He said, "No more talk."

I said, "How's Physics?"

He said, "I'll know when I go back," and disappeared into the tree.

I said, "You okay in there?" but he was gone.

CHAPTER 26

The Last Chance Saloon was off to our right. It was a biker bar, and the parking lot was often filled with cops writing out tickets and making arrests. I'd never been inside, but I knew people who had, and everyone agreed it was the best place to get beat up or hit from behind by a bouncer with a billyclub. The outside was brick. The sign was wood, the paint peeling off. When I drove by the Last Chance Saloon, I always imagined a woman in a black leather bra and jeans dancing on a table so that her high heels clicked on the worn-down wood.

Matt said, "Can we get served there?"

I said, "It's not even eight in the morning."

He said, "That's the kind of place that opens at eight in the morning. It's the only time when guys like us are safe. I bet right now it's packed with old alkies and more old alkies and two women in wigs, smoking menthols at the bar."

I said, "There's no one in the parking lot."

He said, "We could go to the 3 Rs in Youngwood. They open at 7:30 or something for the guys who live in the rooms upstairs. My dad drinks there in the summer."

I said, "At eight in the morning?"

Matt said, "I don't know."

I said, "How much money do you have?"

"I don't know. Twenty bucks, eighteen bucks, something like that. More than enough to get drunk in an old man bar on draft beer. What about you?"

I said, "A little more." Then, "Did you ever think if we saved all the money we spent on beer and fast food, we wouldn't have to rob the paint store to get the money for the abortion?"

He said, "Susan took care of that. She stole that money."

I said, "I know. I'm just saying."

"A case of shit beer is six bucks. Fast food is three bucks, two if you don't get the drink. If we quit spending money on beer and eats, it'd take us twenty-five or thirty weeks to get three hundred dollars. Then guess what?"

"You'd be a dad."

He said, "Fucking right, I'd be a dad." He said, "Now what?"

I said, "Now what, exactly."

I looked at the Last Chance Saloon and tried to open the glass front door with my mind. I willed the bartender to fill two pitchers with Budweiser. I willed the bartender to be a beautiful woman and naked. I waited for her to deliver our beer. She didn't deliver our beer. Our beer was still in a keg, buried somewhere in the cold, damp basement of a biker bar. I went back to using my mind to worry about my mind.

Matt said, "We're not gonna make a great day with thirty-eight fucking bucks, are we?"

I said, "Probably not."

He said, "I have the two-fifty that Susan stole from her mom. I mean, I have it on me right now. In my pocket."

I said, "Two-fifty is about what I would like to spend right now."

He said, "Two fifty is not that much money if you think about it."

I said, "It's probably enough money for a day like today."

"That's about it, though," Matt said.

He didn't know what he was trying to say, and I didn't either, except that we knew.

I said, "I doubt that would be enough to cover anything anyway. I don't want to sound like a know-it-all, but two hundred and fifty dollars doesn't sound like it would cover an abortion. Does it? I'm just saying." I said, "I'm just making up the facts, but I know we're going to need more than three hundred dollars. Probably more like five or six."

Matt said, "Maybe we could pinch a little from her pile, the two-fifty, and do something. Just get away from the whole idea of all this. If it's not enough, it's not enough. We're gonna have to hit the paint store anyway. Right? So why not take a couple bucks for ourselves?"

A car pulled up behind us and beeped. I glanced back, and it was a truck, a big one, loaded down with ladders and house-painting equipment. Two men crowded the front seat. The truck honked again, louder and longer. I'd forgotten we were at a stop sign and not pulled off somewhere. I looked in the sideview mirror. The driver had a huge mustache, a white painters hat turned backwards, and a very red, angry face. He punched the horn again, literally punched it, like he was trying to kill his steering wheel, and the sound was like a siren. The guy in the passenger seat, a twin but bigger, leaned out the window and pounded his own door with his palm so it sounded like a metal drum. He shouted something.

I looked at Matt. He had his arm out the window, and I knew his middle finger was waving on the end of his hand.

I said, "Why would you do that?"

He said, "Fuck them," and punched the gas, his finger still in the air as we raced away.

CHAPTER 27

Al's Tavern opened at seven in the morning if necessary. That's what the sign said: 7 AM (IF NECESSARY), the necessary done in block letters and black magic marker. I'd been there before, usually for six packs, sometimes for a drink at the bar. I didn't know if they would serve Matt, if his long hair added or subtracted years.

One night, instead of buying the usual Old Milwaukee tallboys to go, I ordered a beer and took a stool. The only guy at the bar was a blind man, black-skinned with red freckles. His voice was a croak. He was at least seventy. Huge wrap-around sunglasses covered his eyes, and he hooked a walking cane around his wrist. He wore a handsome beige fedora and old denim overalls, and he kept insisting I looked exactly like his nephew, Jackson Winton III. He was missing teeth, front and sides, but his smile worked. He said, "Jackson, you sound so white," and laughed and dropped his cane, and I picked it up and hooked it back over his wrist. I loved him. We bought each other beers until I thought I might throw up, then I went home. I came back two nights later. I ordered a six pack and stayed for a beer. The same guy was there, but he didn't recognize me. He didn't hear my white voice and say, "You look exactly like my nephew, Jackson Winton III." The bartender that night was ancient. I could have stayed. The blind man might have found me. But two old guys came in, one in a wheelchair, and everyone moved to a table, so I finished my beer and left.

Al's was a dump. I'd been in four other bars, and I knew. It smelled like piss and stale beer. The floor was dirty with pretzel pieces and peanut shells. There were vinyl booths, wobbly tables, and a wooden bar. Metal beer signs lined the walls. The walls were concrete and cinderblock. The jukebox still spun forty-fives. The songs were sung by Hank Williams, Sr., Hank Williams, Jr., and AC/DC.

Two weeks later, I came back. I was drunk when I walked through the door. I went to the jukebox and played "Highway to Hell" twelve times (three dollars worth). I drank a whiskey sour. I drank another. The music was loud. A guy wearing a shoe with a wooden heel walked over to the jukebox and unplugged the cord. He said, "Enough!" but he said it like two words, e and nuff. He was pissed. I thought everyone was pissed. I finished my drink and bought a bag of pretzels and left and didn't plan on coming back.

Now it was 9:07 in the morning, and I knew I could get served, was sure I could get served, but maybe not. It wasn't uncommon for teenagers to drink in the dive bars of Western Pennsylvania back in the 80s, and I'd been shaving since sixth grade, but every time I stepped into a bar, it felt like an audition. Maybe they remembered me at Al's Tavern. Maybe I was a regular and expected, and someone would say, "Where you been?" and buy me a shot of bottom-shelf liquor. But maybe I was a joke. Maybe I was worse than that. I'd been mocked. I'd been banned. Maybe I was the guy who played AC/DC until old men lost their hearing, or I was the guy who let a blind man buy me drinks.

Matt said, "Let's make this a day. Seriously."
I said, "Right."
He said, "We're good at that."

It was true. We had very few talents, but we were gold at spinning nothing into something with only time and a few beers.

We looked at the sign. When, I thought, is it not necessary?

We went back to Matt's car. If we wanted to succeed, we had to be perfect. There was my shirt, and the fact that I'd shaved. I couldn't just grow hair on my chin, but I could change clothes. We swung back towards my house. I changed into cords and a plain oxford shirt. For shoes, docksiders. On my wrist, my dad's Timex, the fancy one he wore to church.

Our plan with this: I would stumble into the bar looking, more or less, like I didn't swing a pick-axe for a living or drive a dump truck into giant ditches for union wages. I'd ask the barkeep or the old alkies (if any were at the bar) if they'd seen Matt. Then I'd describe Matt like I knew him but not really, liked him but not really, never, of course, mentioning his age.

Matt said, "The worst thing they can do is kick us out."

I said, "The worst thing they can do is arrest us."

We were driving the speed limit back into Herminie. My dad's watch was killing me. The metal band pulled at my arm hairs.

Matt said, "How'd you find this place?"

I said, "I went looking."

CHAPTER 28

Herminie was a scratch of a town. The main business was a feed shop that sold autoparts and live rabbits for pets and food. The bank kept limited hours. There was a Laundromat with three washers, two driers, and a broken change machine. Piles of slag, like tiny black mountains, lined the hills, but the mines had been closed for years, and the shafts had all been dynamited. On the hill above Main Street, the houses were made of shingles and rotting lumber. When I was fifteen, and my big brother was leaving for college and I didn't know who was going to buy me beer, he said, "Go to Herminie. They serve anybody." I went to Herminie. They served anybody.

Matt parked on Main Street, two blocks from Al's Tavern, the car angled for the highway if we needed to run.

"Here goes," I said.

Matt said, "Hey." He said, "Don't use my real name."

"If I use a fake name, I'll get confused and fuck it up."

"Use my rock n' roll name."

"What rock n' roll name? When did you get a rock n' roll name?"

Matt said, "The name I'm thinking about using if I stay in rock."

I said, "What name is that?"

He said, "Joe Stalin."

I said, "What?"

He said, "Like the Russian."

I said, "No."

I closed the door. I headed down Main Street, putting my shoes on the sidewalk like I imagined someone twenty-one years of age or older would do until I came to the bricks and rubble that was Al's Tavern.

I started to open the screen door and thought: screen door? Businesses, real businesses like restaurants and pizza shops and video rental stores, didn't have screen doors. I stepped back to make sure I was in the right place. Both windows had neon beer signs, Bud and Miller, but it was daylight so I couldn't be sure if they were lit. I looked for an Open sign. I looked for a Closed sign. I stood on my toes and peeked through the glass. It was dark, foggy. The inside looked blue with smoke.

Someone yelled, "We're open."

I pushed the door. I imagined adult things, houses and wives.

"I thought you were open," I said. "Just peeking to make sure."

The bartender was not Al. Al was old. He was bald. He was skinny with a paunch. He moved slow and wore slippers. This bartender was maybe forty. He had lots of black hair and a camouflage baseball hat on. He was unshaven. There was a green faded tattoo on his neck. His teeth were all brown and crooked, but he smiled, and I thought he looked warm. Warm, meaning not like a serial killer.

The bar was exactly like I remembered it: a bar. Two senior citizens sat at opposite ends of the room, nursing drinks and watching the Today Show on TV.

The bartender said, "Can I help you?"

I said, "Yeah, actually. I'm looking for this guy, Matt Williams, a construction guy."

He said, "I don't think I know any Matt Williams," but he looked interested and not like he was going to ask for my ID.

I said, "He works construction." I said, "Matt Williams."

The bartender glanced over the bar and said, "Yeah, it's mostly medical professionals in here at this hour." He laughed.

I didn't know if I should laugh, too, so I said, "I was supposed to meet him down at the hardware store about half an hour ago, but I'm running late. I thought he might be in here."

The bartender said, "Just Ted and Mikey," and nodded at his regulars, one of whom looked up and raised his drink.

"Okay," I said.

I should have stopped. The lie had worked. But I moved towards the bar and the metal taps that pumped domestic beer, and I said more things that were not true.

I said, "Kind of long-haired guy. He's got this sort of faggoty-girlie hair. Probably dressed in jeans and a t-shirt and some shit-kicking boots. He's supposed to put a porch on for me. A back porch. A deck, I guess."

The bartender said, "Yeah." He said, "Still don't know the guy."

I leaned against the bar like Matt might magically appear, like Mikey or Ted might take off their fishing hats and be Matt. I reached for my wallet and stopped.

Finally, the bartender said, "Well, not many people make it in this early, just the old miners and a few drunk guys."

The man in the hat who had raised his drink said, "I'm an old miner."

The bartender pointed at a stool and said, "Have a seat. It's never too early for a beer."

I said, "Don't twist my arm," and ordered an Esquire draft, one of the three beers they had on tap.

A couple sips later, I looked up as Matt opened the front door.

I said, "Hey." I said, "There you are."

Matt said, "I've been over at the hardware store since nine o'clock. Where you been?" He looked at my beer. He said, "Getting drunk?"

I said, "First beer." I said, "Sorry about that." I said, "I was just over there. I was running late and assumed I missed you." I said, "I thought you might be in here."

He said, "At nine in the morning?"

I said, "It's almost 9:30."

He said, "Buy me a beer, and we'll call it even." He nodded at the bartender and said, "I'll take it off his estimate."

"Sure," I said, admiring the ad-libbed line.

Matt came closer and slapped me on the back and it sounded like a thunderclap and it felt like I'd been hit by a stone, and I didn't know if this was how adult men, professional and laborer, greeted each other.

I said, "Take it easy, big guy," though Matt looked thin as a leg on a barstool.

CHAPTER 29

The bartender had a lot of tattoos, not just the green ink on his neck. He had tattoos on his forearms and biceps and knuckles. His ankles and calves were covered with devils and sea creatures. On his left thigh, he said, was a parrot, more like a toucan, but the beak was too messed up for him to show us.

"This one," he said. He lifted his t-shirt and turned around. "This was the ship I lived on in the Pacific Ocean from 1971-1978."

The shirt came off. He flexed his lats, and there it was: a boat—big, gray, numbered, a battleship with guns firing shells, a black flag with skull-and-crossbones run up the flagpole.

"The Jolly Roger was my idea," he said.

I said, "Wow."

I'd never seen so many tattoos on one person, and I'd been around people with tattoos my whole life. My father had two. My grandfather had one. My uncle had a couple he was ashamed of, especially the half-naked cowgirl. But this guy was covered. Women. Anchors. Hearts. Birds. His mom's name. A bird lifting a heart with his mom's name written inside. He had all the tattoos I'd ever seen and some I hadn't. None of them were very good and most of them had faded to green or gray or an ugly brown, but they were still tattoos, still recognizable as stories. My dad never talked about his tattoos and once, when I asked, he said, "I don't know. I never think about it," and my grandfather said, "Stupid," and my uncle, of course, wore long-sleeved shirts, even in the summer. But our bartender loved his tattoos. He fingered each one, stretching the pictures. He was proud. The marks were his life, a calendar that faded but never got replaced.

It was noon, and we were all buzzed. The old men, Mikey and Ted, had drunk their breakfast beers and gone home for naps. Now it was us, three males of indeterminate ages, and Esquire drafts in plastic pitchers, and pretzels in a brown plastic bowl. Everything was fast. The clock. The drinks. The bartender's name was John, but he'd been in the Navy, so everyone called him Captain. We called him Captain. He treated the tap like an oar on a rowboat, like he was paddling drinks until we were on the shore.

After his forth or fifth beer, Captain turned his ballcap around so he looked like a retired semipro catcher. He sat on his chair backwards. Sometimes he rested his elbows on the chair-back and his chin on his clasped hands to show that he was listening. He didn't appear to notice our ages or care, or he believed our bullshit, or he was lonely and we helped that. I wanted to talk, and I did, but barely. Nothing I knew fit. No one I knew, for example, had gotten his wife's name tattooed on his chest then, after the divorce, scalded off the letters with a hot butter knife. I would have liked to have known someone like that, but I didn't, so I tried to look like I did or that I might someday be that person.

"Oh shit," Captain said. "Look at this one," and he started lifting his shirt again.

I said, "Come on, Captain, you showed us the tugboat already."

"Not the boat," he said. "The woman. Right here."

He pointed to his side, and there it was: a Japanese woman's face. I guessed she was a geisha. Or maybe a concubine. I'd seen *Shogun* on TV, but it was late and I'd fallen asleep. I remembered the fight scenes, the men and their Samurai swords, but the women were distant. The women were delicate. They listened to the men and loved them. I guessed they were prostitutes but with silk robes and tiny feet. The woman on Captain's ribs had a flower in her hair. She was fanning herself—or hiding herself—with a paper fan. The color wasn't great, but the geisha's robe was orange or peach, something new, and it was the best tattoo he'd shown us.

I said, "Who's that? Like a Japanese whore or something?"

Matt said, "She looks like Julia Roberts but Chinese."

Captain looked at Matt and said, "I don't know what the hell that means."

Matt said, "Julia Roberts. She was the hooker in *Pretty Woman*."

Captain angled his neck to see his side and said, "I don't know. I can't see Julia Roberts there." He said, "Maybe an oriental Heather Locklear, but that's about it." He said, "Anyway, this tattoo is a genuine representation of a Korean prostitute from the Lo Cho district as illustrated by a Japanese tattoo artist who didn't understand a word of fucking English." Captain let his shirt drop and smiled with his brown cracked teeth. He said, "I think it turned out pretty fucking good, considering."

I said, "That's the funniest thing I've ever heard."

Captain said, "Tell me."

Matt said, "What the hell were you doing in Japan?"

Captain said, "R and R. I got drunk. I had this picture of this Korean whore that I had been spending a lot of time with back in Pusan, and I thought: well, why not. I'll get her pretty young Korean mug tattooed right here on my side, and when I get back to Korea, she'll keep the free pussy coming."

I said, "What does that mean: free pussy?"

Matt said, "Right." He said, "The whores I sleep with all take my money."

I went to my beer and thought: the whores I sleep with? Matt was a wonderful liar, better than I had known. He really was a maker of porches, a man of heavy machinery.

Captain said, "In Korea, the whores all give it away free to the American GIs. It's part of the trip, you know. Anyway, I was in Japan. I was all fucked-up on sake, rice wine shit, prune whiskey if you can believe it, just awful stuff, and I'd been getting inked about once a month for almost a year by then and, frankly, I was running out of ideas. Not all these tats I'm showing you are first fucking rate." He picked up a pretzel. He put it down without taking a bite. He said, "So I'm drunk as hell and I remember this picture of my Korean ho that I keep in my wallet, and I just figure fuck it. Why not, you know. I wasn't going to marry her, so fuck it, it was the least I could do, right?"

I said, "You could have just paid her."

Captain said, "Well, hindsight is to a drinker what a crystal ball is to a fortuneteller—you know what the fuck I'm talking about?" He laughed and rocked so far back on his chair that he almost tipped. He said, "Whooo," and righted himself. He said, "Back then, I thought I'd be living on whores, sake, and sticky rice for the rest of my life." He said, "If I would have known I was going to live this long, I would have taken better care of myself. Mickey Mantle said that. Maybe Babe Ruth. I hate baseball."

I looked at Matt and raised my beer. The glass looked short and chubby with a wide mouth at the top. Matt raised his own glass and held it there.

Captain said, "I haven't had a good toast in ages. Let me get in on that." He drained his beer from a mug with his name written on the side and filled it again from the pitcher. He said, "I sure am glad you two stumbled in here today. I don't know if I could have taken another day of the afternoon soaps."

"To General Hospital," Matt said.

"To Susan Lucci," I said.

"Wrong soap," Captain said. "But a good try." He raised his new beer. He said, "This is for you two young gentlemen. High seas and low women."

We all clinked glasses.

Captain finished his beer in a sip and said, "I'm gonna be honest."

I said, "Okay."

Matt said, "Honest about what?"

Captain said, "Honest-honest."

I waited. I could feel Matt waiting. Captain adjusted his shoulders like there was something in there, a squirrel or a rat. So he knew our ages. It was obvious now. But then it was obvious before. Nothing mattered after all these drinks. Captain was my best friend. If he tried to arrest me, I was going to break my glass over his head.

He said, "I have the cancer. I don't tell anyone. I don't make a big deal out of it. It's just the way it is, and I thought you two guys should know who you're drinking with."

He nodded, one time at each of us, like he was giving us something with his face.

I was intensely relieved that we were talking about cancer and not under-aged drinking.

Then I wasn't.

I said, "I'm sorry to hear that."

Matt said, "My grandma had cancer." He said, "But she's better now." He said, "I guess she could still get worse." He said, "I'm sorry, too." He looked towards the jukebox.

Captain said, "It's okay."

I said, "It's not though."

Matt said, "Shit."

Captain said, "Really. I'm fine with it. I just wanted you guys to know. You've both been awfully kind to me today, sitting around here, drinking and listening to my stupid stories, when I know you have better things to do."

I said, "Your stories aren't stupid."

Matt said, "Yeah."

Captain said, "Okay then."

But it was like the room had cancer now, the whole bar. Captain had infected everything with his confession, and now we were going to die with him. I wasn't ready. I didn't want cancer. I wanted more beer and tattoos. This had all been so great.

Captain said, "I should piss," and stood. He checked his legs to see if they still walked and stepped to the restroom.

I turned to Matt and mouthed: what?

Matt whispered, "Is he crazy or great?"

I didn't know. The bar was so quiet we could hear Captain's stream hitting the toilet then water splashing in the sink. I filled everyone's glasses with beer. The sound of the towel dispenser was like a storm made of dented metal and paper. I hoped Captain wasn't dying in there. If he was, I'd need to go in there and maybe die, too.

Matt said, "Should we leave?"

I didn't know. I put my finger to my lips. We couldn't be as loud as the restroom.

Captain came back to the table. I looked at him and didn't know if he liked to be looked at, if my eyes were embarrassing him. I waved and turned away. He touched the back of my head. It was only a second, less than a second, but it was like a massage, like a bolt of slow lightening had enter my body and calmed me down. Captain leaned on a chair but he didn't sit. The chair wobbled. Captain quit leaning. He adjusted his baseball hat. The hat said something about the Army, the slogan splattered in paint.

Captain smiled and said, "I don't know why I said that. I don't have cancer. I'm fine as a fucking canary." He said, "Who filled up my beer?" He said, "Thanks be to one of you." He drank. Then he pulled his body to attention and saluted us.

CHAPTER 30

The cancer was gone. Either it was a joke or not. I took a drink and looked over my beer glass at Captain and all his ink, his ships and women, and I understood. There had been cancer, truly, but Captain had confessed it and stood and wobbled to the restroom and pissed, and he had healed himself. Nothing had been a lie. It had been a miracle, and now he looked huge in his life, and I felt puny in mine. I was seventeen, and I couldn't heal myself. My cancer was years away. I didn't have any tattoos. I'd never drunk sake. I'd never been on a boat or fucked a Korean whore. Maybe I'd never be in the Navy. I wasn't going to Japan today, not from Al's Tavern in Herminie, Pennsylvania. Whatever needed saving was saved or could not be saved from here. Fine. It was tattoos then. I'd always wanted a dragon.

If I left the bar and walked into a tattoo parlor, I would remember this day and these exact beers and the way the pretzels crumbled and how Hank Williams, Sr. played on the jukebox even though nobody dropped a quarter, and how brave Matt was in the face of fatherhood, and how I was his best friend, how I planned everything, and how we had witnessed a miracle, and it would be vivid like this forever, even if the ink faded like it had on Captain.

"Where exactly," I said, "would a person get a tattoo around here?"

Captain said, "A person like you?"

I said, "Sure."

Matt said, "A person like me, too." He looked at his watch, a big metal thing with an even bigger black leather band. He said, "Shit, I guess I'm not working today."

"No kidding," I said. "I should probably call the office."

Matt said, "I always thought I'd get a tiger, something fierce, right here on my forearm."

I said, "I always thought I'd get a bulls-eye, right here, on my forehead." I pointed my finger and screwed it like an arrow into my forehead.

Then Captain got serious. He did some gestures, rearranged the beer and pretzels. I didn't want it to be cancer again. If it was cancer again, I would have to take him to the hospital because he couldn't be Jesus twice, and I would have to save him, like I was saving Matt by getting him drunk in the afternoon.

"You, I can see with a tattoo," Captain said and nodded at Matt. "You got that fucked-up Heather Thomas hair and your own construction business. That's tattoo stuff." Then he looked at me. He said, "You, and I'm not judging, I'm just saying, it might not be right for you." He said, "Don't make any bad decisions. I knew a lot of young guys when I was in the Navy, and they all came in and started getting tattoos, but in four years, when their time was up and they were thinking about going to college on the GI Bill or whatever, they knew they were fucked." He said, "You can't be a dentist and be covered in tattoos. You'll scare the teeth and gums." He looked at me like he wanted to hire me or take me to war but I'd failed something, flunked a test, and he couldn't.

I said, "What am I, a fucking fag?"

Captain laughed and said, "That's not what I'm saying."

I looked both ways. I opened my mouth wide and checked to see if it was filled. I stood up and turned around and took a good look at my own ass, and said, "There's not any cocks coming out of me, is there?" I swatted at my butt like there might have been a penis hanging there. I opened my mouth again. I stretched out my cheeks with two fingers. I said, "Nope, no cocks in there."

Captain said, "Okay, stop. I'm not calling anyone a poof. I'm just saying. Be smart. You look like you have a good job. You're getting a fucking porch on your house. You don't need any tattoos messing that up. Look at me. I walk into a job interview, and they think I'm Charlie Manson. These tattoos might as well say: convicted killer. I love my ink, but it don't make my life easy." He took off his camo hat, messed his hair, then put the cap back on, facing front.

I said, "A little one." I said, "Up on my shoulder."

I felt like I was talking to my dad, some better version who understood tattoos and reason and beer and why it was important to heal your own cancer.

Captain said, "A little one."

Matt said, "I'll make sure."

Captain said, "Nothing on your neck or your knuckles."

I said, "My shoulder, that's it."

He said, "Well." He said, "I ain't exactly a fucking role model."

Matt said, "Sure you are."

Captain said, "God save us." He went to the bar for another pitcher. When he came back, his other hand held a tablet and a tiny yellow pencil. He set down the beer. He pointed the pencil at me and said, "On your shoulder, that's it," and then he printed the directions to Charlie Chan's Tattoo Emporium so that the words looked like they had been written by a very young child.

CHAPTER 31

When I was eight years old, I found a twenty dollar bill in the parking lot of Tom's Arco. I didn't tell my mom. She was inside, paying off Tom for repair work he'd done on our Gremlin's air conditioning. Tom was a crook, and my dad hated him, but it was summer, and the few other garages in the area were booked. My mom wanted the AC fixed. The seats in the Gremlin were black vinyl, and she had small children who were burning their legs and crying. My dad said, "Fine. Whatever."

I stuffed the twenty in my front pocket. I don't know what I wanted to do with it. Buy candy. Maybe a tape from K-Mart or Hills. My dad was laid off. My mom was talking about finding a job, something part-time, and weeping. I took the twenty and hid it in my bedroom.

Later that night, I heard my dad shouting about the price Tom had charged my mom for the air conditioning. It hadn't needed repaired. It had only needed charged. My dad's voice was loud enough to lock my bedroom door.

The next day, my mom found the twenty. She asked me about it, and then we returned to Tom's Arco where I handed over the money like a thief. Tom was a fat man but he was solid. He had dark black hair piled on his head like Elvis. The tips of his fingers were greasy and his knuckles were covered in kinky black hair. He wore gray pants that were surprisingly clean and a blue work shirt that wouldn't hang down over his fat hairy belly.

Tom said, "I'll ask around and see if anybody lost anything."

I waited for a reward, at least five bucks, or, like my mom had suggested, for Tom to let me keep the bill because no one had come back to ask for it.

Tom put the money in his front pocket and said, "Air conditioning, right? How's that working out for you? Nice and cool now?"

My mom said, "Well, thank you."

Tom said, "No problem."

I didn't want to say anything, but I did.

I said, "There goes my twenty bucks," and my mom slapped me.

We stepped outside of Al's Tavern and I saw a penny on the ground. I picked it up. Matt was too drunk and happy to notice, but I did what I always did when I found money, even a penny on the ground: I thought about Tom and my mom, my dad and our Gremlin, my twenty bucks and the way it disappeared like a magic trick.

Every idea is based on an idea. My dad knew what he was doing when he let my mom go to Tom's Arco. My mom knew what she was doing when she forced me to give back the money. Tom knew what he was doing when he snatched it with his fat greasy hand.

I thought about Susan. Stealing money from a pile of stolen money was not smart, especially when the plan was to steal more money to replace the money we were about to steal from the pile of stolen money.

I had the directions to the tattoo parlor folded neatly in my hand.

I put the penny in my pocket. We went.

CHAPTER 32

On Route 136, near Beaver Road, Matt pulled his Nova to the edge of the road. The dirt and gravel pinged the underneath of the car. Matt turned on the hazard lights. The lights clicked like a metronome, two arrows flashing on the dashboard. I spun around to make sure we weren't being followed. I didn't know by whom. A school bus, empty, blew by on the left. No one else was on the road. Matt opened the door. He leaned outside and puked. It wasn't a lot of puke, only a second or two of gagging. He spit and closed the door.

He said, "Fucking pretzels."

I said, "You want me to drive?"

He said, "I'm fine."

CHAPTER 33

Down the road, Matt reached across me and popped open the glove compartment. He ruffled through some papers, old bills, the manual. The sun outside was blinding. He took out a bottle of pills. He said, "I almost forgot about these."

I said, "What are those?"

He said, "These are uppers. I found them in Susan's mom's purse."

He handed me the bottle.

I said, "There's only three."

Matt said, "I know, and they're tiny."

He took one.

I took two.

CHAPTER 34

The driveway to Charlie Chan's Tattoo Emporium was at least a mile long, maybe longer, and most of the asphalt had been stripped away. What remained was dirt, rocks, and potholes. On Route 136, Matt had been a racecar driver, but now he snailed along at five miles per hour, swerving to avoid the larger divots, sometimes stopping then easing the Nova through a small trench or over a mud-packed hump. Finally, he moved the car off the road and onto the grass so that the ride was less bumpy, but small tree branches scraped the windows and doors.

Matt said, "I'm totally fucking up my paint job."

He gently maneuvered back onto the road. Off in the distance, we spotted Charlie Chan's trailer and a wooden sign advertising tattoos. It was exactly as Captain had described it: single-wide, up on cinder blocks; a long wooden porch that had been stained red and black; a fancy dragon painted on the front door. A detached garage was off to the left, and the same dragon had been stenciled onto the side of the building.

Charlie Chan answered the door before we could knock. He was shirtless and shoeless. He wore loose sweatpants and two wristbands, one red, one black. He was, as we'd expected, covered in tats. But we hadn't expected him to be Italian with short dark hair. Charlie Chan looked like he'd been rehearsing to play a guy who grew up in the Bronx. He was thin, but heavily muscled, and stood at a cocky angle. He looked younger than Captain, but it was hard to tell with all those muscles and tattoos.

"Yo," he said, and bowed politely. He said, "Gentlemen, what's up?" and he shook our hands. He bowed again. This was all very friendly and natural. The cockiness—the edges—instantly disappeared. He said, "Captain called ahead. Come on in. Make yourself at home." He rubbed his own short black hair like he was petting a friendly dog. He said, "I'm running a little behind this morning. Rough night, you know."

I said, "I know that."

Matt said, "Me, too."

We didn't say that it was afternoon. I looked at Charlie Chan's arms. He needed a watch, not wrist bands.

He said, "This way, you guys," and led us towards the back bedroom. In the hallway, he stopped, extended his muscled arms until his palms braced against the wall, and lifted himself off the floor. He hung there a minute. He dropped down and said, "I used to be able to do an iron cross. I'm outta fucking shape."

I said, "That's impressive. I couldn't do a cartwheel right now."

He said, "Keeps me loose. Lots of sitting when you do tattoos."

He did another hanging thing in the doorway, pulling up his knees into crunches then swinging his torso to work his obliques. For his dismount, he performed a lavish front kick. Matt bumped me with his shoulder. I knew. There was nothing to be scared of, but we were scared. Charlie Chan turned and bowed. I wished I had a beer. I wished I was watching this—Charlie Chan—on TV in some weird Olympics. My mouth was dry. The speed we'd taken hadn't kicked. I grabbed onto the doorframe, inhaled, and busted out ten quick pull-ups. I hung for a second then I started to swing. I didn't nail the front-kick dismount, but I didn't eat carpet or bust a lamp either.

"Nice," Charlie said.

Matt said, "Yeah, I should probably take a pass on that," and stepped into the room, staring up at the doorframe like it was a magnet that attracted idiots and kung fu experts.

Charlie Chan said, "I would train every second of every day if I could." He said, "You guys know." He said, "You guys lift?" He said, "I'd rather spar, but I lift." He said, "You guys know." He said, "Sparring is where it's at." He said, "I do not mind taking a beating."

Charlie Chan was a talker. The words came fast. The words were positive. Charlie Chan loved his own story. His story was a circle, not a line. I figured he was on speed, his fat sister's diet pills, an endless prescription's worth, or some over-the-counter drugs he'd crushed up and combined himself.

Or maybe it was better than that.

I'd heard about cocaine. I'd seen Al Pacino huff up piles in *Scarface*. But I'd never tried it or even knew anyone who had. But I'd thought about it. But I wanted to. I dreamed about it and even wrote a poem with the lines, "somebody give me sweet cocaine / I'm so tired of my sane brain." Cocaine was in the movies, practically starred in the movies, the best ones, *Scarface* and *Less Than Zero*, and even though it might get you killed like it did Pacino or turn you gay like it did Robert Downey, Jr., the high was, apparently, worth it. Cocaine was glamorous and fun and Cubans in Florida and teenagers in Hollywood inhaled it for breakfast. We—Matt and I and our teenage friends and the few young adults we partied with—had beer and pills and, during desperate times, glue. Charlie Chan looked glamorous. Charlie Chan could have been played by Al Pacino or even Robert Downey, Jr. if they did their sit-ups and learned karate. Charlie Chan was not on glue and beer.

Whatever he had, I wanted.

Money was not a problem, but I didn't know the etiquette. Maybe it was acceptable to ask Charlie Chan the price of what he was on because he was twitching like he'd plugged himself into an electrical outlet. Or maybe it was unacceptable because the veins in his neck were as thick as cigars and he was about to pop.

I said, "How many cups of coffee did you wake up to?"

Charlie Chan laughed and said, "Coffee won't do it anymore."

That was fine, open and honest as a beer bottle, but before I could ask about buying his drugs, Charlie wanted to tell us his life story.

He said, "You're probably wondering about the Charlie Chan thing."

Matt said, "Not really."

I said, "A little."

Charlie Chan said, "Captain has some fucked-up tats, huh?" He went back to randomly straightening the room. He said, "I offered to touch up some of the better ones, like the geisha-whore thing on his side, but most of those old ones need covered." He picked up a stack of magazines, shuffled the order. He said, "So, yeah, the whole Charlie Chan thing," and circled back to his original thought. Each of his stories held a story, and the timing of those stories and their relationship to each other fell from Charlie Chan's brain and into his mouth and out into the trailer like raindrops falling from clouds.

Charlie Chan said, "Well what did Captain say about me? Nothing? Okay then." He said, "Here goes. Stop me if you've heard anything."

Charlie Chan had changed his name from Mark Graft after studying the ancient art of skin beautification (his words) in Japan with a man who called himself Master Duk.

"Master Duk, right? D-U-K. Pronounced Do. You guys know. They probably teach that shit in college now. Japanese pronunciation and etcetera. So yeah, Master Duk, pronounced Do. Weird name for a weird dude."

Charlie Chan knew Captain because they had played on the same softball team for three years. They'd bonded over their love of ink. On Charlie Chan's back was a portrait of Jesus, thorny crown and all. A dragon crept over his right shoulder. Both arms were sleeves of color, an orange koi fish on his right, a red-and-black tiger on his left.

Charlie Chan said, "Did you see Captain's tugboat?" He said, "Ouch." He said, "Great guy, but seriously, ouch." He said, "Unless you guys are thinking about getting your legs tattooed and want to see my work, I'll keep my pants on." He said, "Master Duk was insane. But in a good way. The guy had his eyelids tattooed."

I said, "I'm thinking about my shoulder."

I was afraid Charlie Chan was going to drop his sweatpants.

Matt said, "I like your tiger."

Charlie Chan said, "I do bamboo tattoos, too. You name it."

Matt said, "Really?" like he knew what a bamboo tattoo was. It'd barely been six months since he'd had his ear pierced with a second stud at Spencer's Gifts.

Charlie Chan said, "Scarifacation. Piercings. You name it. I'm not saying I have a license to do it. I'm saying I do it. This is ancient shit in Japan, but it's all new to America. In ten years, you'll see businessmen with badass brands, tattoos on their necks, tattooed neckties maybe, chicks with their pussies pierced, nipples pierced, rings tattooed on their fingers. It's endless once this stuff takes off. We are gonna be a painted people."

Charlie Chan kept talking, sometimes pausing to give himself an intense arm massage. Matt and I listened. When he pointed at one of his tattoos, we complimented it. We complimented the room, the way it had been decorated. We liked the Japanese paintings, the warriors especially, but we liked the guy with the flute too. The Japanese flag tacked to the ceiling was both eerie and respectful. Matt liked the red track lighting. I liked the white lamp that shined down on the barber's chair where we would get marked.

Charlie Chan said, "I shouldn't even have to say this but, obviously, I use clean needles. That's my sterilizer right there. All the ink is fresh. I never double dip. I do everything top notch. A lot of my business is repeat customers who like what I've done. This isn't some shitty sailor joint where drunk guys get Mom tattooed on their foreheads." He said,

"Okay, here's my books. These are the tats that I've done or can do no problem. I'll leave you guys alone to decide. If you have any questions, I'll be in the kitchen." He said, "I need to hit it one more time or get something to eat or something. I'm fucking worn out."

Matt and I said, "Cool."

Binders, at least thirty, some stacked, some straightened like books, filled a black metal shelf against the wall. We started on the far left and flipped through the pages.

Down the hall, Charlie Chan banged pots and pans in the kitchen, slamming cabinet doors and opening the refrigerator, until we smelled bacon cooking and maybe eggs.

I wondered if he'd hit it again.

I wondered what it was, and if it was for sale, and if I could hit some too.

CHAPTER 35

Charlie Chan said, "Look, I don't want to be sneaking around in my own place. You guys want to do a line or two?"

I closed the binder and said, "I could do a line."

Matt said, "Just to take the edge off."

Charlie Chan said, "Come on in the kitchen and don't touch my bacon. Never touch a man's bacon."

The kitchen was a tiny clean room with flowered canisters and a cookie jar shaped like a pear on top on the counter. The walls were yellow. The table was a small square covered with a clean green cloth. Over the sink was a painting of three ducks, happily waddling by a pond. The bacon was on a plate covered with a paper towel. The eggs were in the pan, a slice of American cheese resting on the pile.

Charlie Chan opened a cabinet and pulled down a mirror the size of an album cover. There were four lines already cut, lined up like white roads. The mirror was dusty with coke and the coke had been smeared in places and there were fingerprints. Charlie set everything on the kitchen table, like a housewife setting out snacks.

He said, "You guys go ahead. I'm onto breakfast."

I said, "You sure?"

He picked up a piece of bacon and bit it in half.

Matt said, "Go ahead, Dan. It's all you."

I thought Charlie Chan would hand me a straw or something but he didn't, so I pulled out a dollar bill and started to roll it up, just like Tony Montana in *Scarface*, something I had never done before and something I immediately wanted to do again.

I did a line. Matt did a line. Neither of us had a stroke. Our hearts did not collapse. We switched nostrils and did the other two lines.

Charlie Chan said, "That was fast. You young guys don't mess around."

Matt said, "Not that young."

Charlie Chan said, "I'm not that old. Just semi-old." He said, "I don't know why I love bacon. It's terrible for me."

I tilted my head and rubbed my nose. The taste in my throat was terrible, like chalk and aspirin, but the rest was great. I was ready. I wanted more lines, more beers. I wanted to trade skins with Charlie Chan and wear all those tattoos from around the world. I wanted to do flying kicks. Lots of flying kicks and lots of cocaine.

I said, "Do you have more we can buy?"

Matt said, "Yeah, really."

Charlie Chan said, "Let's see how much your tattoos cost. That's my business. This stuff is just for fun and etcetera. You guys know."

CHAPTER 36

The prices were unbelievably reasonable. The choices were abundant.

Matt said, "I should get one of each."

He passed me the next binder. I closed the one I'd been looking through.

All the designs had left us confused. Charlie Chan could have said, "A dragon for you, a scorpion for you," and we would have extended our arms and given him our money.

I looked at Tweety Bird. I knew someone, a girl, with a Tweety Bird. It was not a cool tattoo. It was yellow and happy. I looked at the Tasmanian Devil. I looked at the Tasmanian Devil holding a beer can. There he was again, strangling Elmer Fudd.

Matt said, "I don't even know. Probably stay away from the Looney Tunes."

I said, "I don't even care. I just want something."

He said, "Yeah."

I whispered, "We have to get more coke."

Matt said, "I've never been so happy in my whole life."

I said, "Me, too."

Matt said, "I wish I had my bass. I could just sit here and thump the strings."

I said, "I don't know why I don't play guitar."

Matt said, "You totally should. You should absolutely play guitar."

Charlie Chan yelled from the kitchen, "How you guys doing back there?"

I said, "Still looking. Maybe ten more minutes."

Charlie Chan said, "Take your time." He said, "You guys want some bacon?"

I said, "No thanks."

He said, "I'm making the rest of the pack."

I said, "We're good."

I could feel our voices moving through the hall like roommates, like old friends.

Matt said, "That dude loves bacon."

I went back to the binder.

I said, "Are you sure these are the prices?"

Matt said, "I think so." Then, "How much for some more coke?"

I shrugged.

Matt said, "We should be quiet."

I said, "We're whispering."

Matt said, "My tongue is numb. It's doing something to my ears."

CHAPTER 37

Charlie Chan walked in with the mirror.

He said, "You guys can finish this up."

It was the same mirror as before. No new lines had been added.

He said, "You know, polish the gums."

He ran his finger across the glass and stuck it in his mouth like it was a toothbrush. He handed me the mirror and went back to the kitchen and the rest of the bacon.

I looked at Matt. Before I could suggest something or shrug or look confused or make like Charlie Chan and rub my gums with the powder, Matt bent towards the mirror like he was about to do an invisible line then he licked the glass. He came up and there was a line of slobber.

I said, "Why did you do that?"

He said, "It feels good on my tongue."

CHAPTER 38

I decided I would get a rose on my shoulder. I had reasons. First, I liked the size, small, and the color, the way the red was almost purple in places. Second, Paul Stanley from KISS had the same tattoo. It gave me a certain confidence knowing a rock star had picked the same thing. Third, the rose was only fifteen bucks. That meant we'd have lots of extra money for drugs. Maybe a trash bag filled with coke. Maybe a freezer bag. Maybe it would buy us four more lines or just another lick on the mirror.

Matt picked out a black panther. It was forty-five bucks. I thought that was greedy. Whatever drugs we did buy, he'd have to take less.

I stuck my head into the hallway. Charlie Chan was at the kitchen table eating eggs and watching a tiny TV that hadn't been there before.

He said, "Give me two seconds to wash up."

I said, "No problem."

Matt whispered, "Is he still tweaking?"

I said, "Does it matter?"

Matt said, "He's cool as shit."

CHAPTER 39

Charlie Chan walked into the room carrying a small Styrofoam cooler filled with ice and green cans of 12 Horse Ale. He pulled on a pair of surgical gloves and started to organize his inks. The inks looked like tiny plastic jars of paint.

Matt said, "Does it hurt?"

Charlie Chan said, "Not unless you're getting your nuts tattooed."

It hurt, but more than that, it sounded like it hurt. It was more like getting sewed by a Singer sewing machine than being tattooed with a needle. There was a device, like a Star Trek phaser, and a pedal on the floor that controlled the speed, and the constant sound of something sharp moving fast enough to mark my skin. After a minute, when I realized my arm wasn't being sawed off at the shoulder, I didn't mind the sound. I think I liked the pain.

Matt said, "So?"

I'd been sweating beer and drugs and happiness. My shirt and t-shirt were piled in the corner. Every few minutes, the tattoo needle would go over a nerve and my chest would flex on its own, and I would have to keep myself from smiling in the mirror.

Charlie Chan said, "You okay?"

I said, "Good."

There was bleeding but he wiped me so often I couldn't tell how much. When he finished the outline and stopped to find the next color, I reached for my beer and took a long cold sip.

Charlie Chan dipped the needle and said, "Ready?"

Matt said, "Why aren't you crying?"

I said, "Because it doesn't hurt."

I was done in twenty minutes. Charlie Chan opened a jar of salve and rubbed my shoulder. He asked how I felt. I felt great. I could have done another tattoo, a bigger one.

"I thought it'd be worse," I said.

"You're tough," he said and screwed the cap back on the salve.

I was still shirtless, flexing my arm in the mirror so I could better see my new rose.

I said, "I love it."

Charlie Chan said, "It's a great first tattoo. You can stop there or add to it forever."

Matt said, "It looks awesome." He said, "Now let's do me before I puke. All that buzzing noise coming from the needle was getting me in the stomach."

Matt took off his shirt, tossed it in the corner, and sat in the chair. He rubbed his face like he was trying to wake up but he was the opposite of sleep.

Charlie Chan said, "Breathe. You'll be fine."

Matt said, "I thought it was going to be a needle. That thing looks like a gun."

Charlie Chan touched his foot to the pedal and the needle started up again, making those sounds that were making Matt sick.

Matt said, "Hold on one second," and jumped from the chair like he was on a bus and suddenly this was his stop.

Charlie Chan said, "Whoo!" He said, "A little more warning next time," and leaned back on his stool and stopped the needle. He said, "Seriously, man, I don't want to nick you."

"No," Matt said, three steps away. "We don't want that."

CHAPTER 40

Charlie said, "Make sure you guys tell your friends. I do the best work in town, and I have the best prices, too. I work out of my home and it's better for everyone."

He stopped and wiped the needle. He took a clean rag across Matt's arm. Matt was quiet. I hoped he wasn't sick, but I knew he was. Charlie Chan knew, too. He stood and took off his plastic gloves and walked from the room. Matt barely moved. He closed his eyes. He breathed in, he breathed out. When I walked over and touched his back, he didn't speak.

I said, "You want a towel? You're soaked."

He said, "Where my shirt?"

I handed him his t-shirt. He wiped his face. He closed his eyes again. I looked at the outline of the tiger. I looked at Matt and the tiger together. I looked at Matt and the tiger together in the mirror. Matt's muscles were more cut than mine but there were less of them and he was too nauseas to keep them flexed.

I said, "You okay?"

Charlie Chan came back with a wet hand towel. He wiped Matt's face and shoulders, his neck and the arm that wasn't being tattooed.

Charlie Chan said, "How's that feel?"

Matt said, "Better, thanks."

"We'll cool you off for a minute."

Charlie Chan washed his hands in the corner sink. He dried them and put on a new pair of gloves. He talked about a chick getting flames tattooed on her pussy lips. "Six sessions," he said. "For an itty-bitty tattoo. She did not handle the pain well." He touched Matt again and said, "You're doing great, man. Hang in there."

Matt said, "Was the chick worse than me?"

Charlie Chan said, "Absolutely." He said, "You get weird spots, like right on the ankle bone, and I've seen bikers cry. Not that I'm very impressed with bikers."

Matt said, "Thanks."

Charlie Chan picked up the needle and said, "Ready?"

Matt said, "I guess." He said, "Yeah." He said, "Go."

Charlie Chan said, "It's the sound. Don't worry about it." He started again. He said, "These American tattoo guys, they're all fucking bikers. You guys know. If you want to work in their shops, you have to start sweeping floors or something. For fucking free. No way. Not when I can ink circles around these dudes. I didn't spend all the money I'd saved while I was in the Army to go to Japan and come back here and run for coffee and sandwiches for some guy who thinks owning a ten-grand motorcycle makes him cool. Fuck that."

Matt said, "It's really starting to hurt again."

The panther on his forearm was large enough to swallow my rose.

Charlie Chan said, "Take a big breath. You're almost done." He backed off the needle, took Matt by the hand, and said, "Man, you'll never be the same."

CHAPTER 41

We stood by the front door. My shirt was tucked in my back pocket like a rag. I had a wife-beater on so I could study my rose which was puffy and a little bloody and supposed to be covered in gauze. Matt was shirtless, his tattoo not covered either. We were both glossy with salve, and we promised Charlie Chan we would bandage our tattoos as soon as we got home. He understood. "First tattoos are miracles," he said.

We'd done more coke. It was a little bag but when Charlie Chan dumped it out and smashed it up, it felt enormous. That was fifty bucks. The other two bags, the ones we'd bought for the road, were forty each.

Charlie Chan said, "I probably shouldn't have tooted that with you. I'm twitchy again. I hate twitchy. I need to start meditating again."

I said, "Omm."

He said, "I know, but it works. I didn't drink for a whole year once. Twelve months, nothing. Not a drop. I ran five miles every day and I meditated. I was a healthy motherfucker." He said, "Shit. Hold on."

He took off down the hall. I thought he might come back with a new drug, something better than coke, something to make my life even brighter.

Matt said, "He's awesome." He said, "My new band is going to be named Charlie Chan."

Charlie Chan came back with a couple coupons. The coupons were hand-printed then Xeroxed and cut into squares. He said, "It's ten percent off. If you guys come back with a couple friends, I'll do your next ones for fifty percent off. That's like one of you for free."

I said, "Alright."

Matt said, "Thanks."

"Hey," Charlie Chan said. "Don't mention to Captain that I sold you blow. He gets weird about that stuff sometimes."

"No problem," I said, and thought about Captain who had been my best friend, and maybe dying with cancer, and now he was nothing compared to Charlie Chan.

CHAPTER 42

We could have walked. Charlie Chan had given us our coupons and we had promised to return. Friendships had been made. Drugs had been purchased and consumed. I had knocked down a vase that had a kamikaze headband tied around it like a bow, and it had not broken. The 12 Horse Ale was gone. I'd hugged Charlie Chan, then Charlie had hugged Matt, then I'd hugged Matt, and Charlie had hugged us both. The moment had come, we'd all seen the moment, it was great, it was lasting, and nobody knew how to finish it off.

Then some fat bald lunatic, wearing sweatpants and a Steelers' jersey with the sleeves cut off, pushed his way through the front door.

Charlie Chan said, "Fat Henry, I wish you would have knocked."

Fat Henry said, "Why's that? So you could have prepared some jujitsu shit for me?"

Charlie said, "No, so I could have locked the fucking door."

Fat Henry said, "Bullshit."

Charlie said, "Really."

Fat Henry had tattoos on both arms. There was the Grim Reaper. There was a wizard. There were dozens of skulls, some flaming, some stabbed with daggers. He had a rain cloud with a lightening bolt. He had a skeleton drinking a martini. The theme was death and debauchery. The ink was black with a few red spots, mostly blood, some of it dripping off a scythe.

Fat Henry said, "All that gook learning has gone to your head, Charlie Chan. My American money is still good here."

Charlie said, "I wish you wouldn't call it gook learning."

Fat Henry said, "Gook learning is what is." He said, "Wisdom, right?" and snorted like he was going to spit.

Charlie said, "Henry, how drunk are you?"

Henry said, "Barely," but when he tried to stand straight, he stumbled and had to grab at the door. He was sweaty, and I could smell the smoke and the beer from five feet away. Fat Henry looked like a professional wrestler, an old-fashioned heel, a heel that had been fired from the league for doing too many bad things when bad things were what he was paid to do.

Charlie said, "One more time: how drunk?"

Henry said, "Two days."

I hadn't known people measured their drunks in days, not bottles.

I turned to Charlie Chan and said, "Thanks again," and reached for his hand.

Matt said, "Yeah, thanks. I love it. Great work Awesome."

We moved towards the door but Fat Henry blocked our exit. He hadn't noticed us before, or cared to notice us, and now he did. He was enormous, more like a fantastic animal. I thought I smelled piss. His nostrils were caked with blood and snot. I stepped back, then forward, then back. Matt retreated three full steps.

Fat Henry said, "Shit, Charlie Chan, I didn't know you were tattooing faggots. Lookie, that one has a rose on his shoulder. Why didn't you tell him that one was for a girlie?"

He made some kissy-faces at me, and I nodded like I was about to do something. I didn't know what. Cry. Get beat up. Matt felt what I was thinking, trying to think, and we moved.

Charlie Chan said, "Pay no attention to the fat man behind the curtain." He said, "Seriously, Fat Henry, step aside." He looked more disgusted than angry.

Fat Henry said, "Yeah?"

Charlie Chan said, "Yeah."

I waited for a kick, a roundhouse, or even a chop, but Henry leaned away from the door. Charlie Chan reached out and shook my hand.

He said, "Seriously, thank you both. You need one or the other, you come back. And tell your friends if they have money. About the one, not the other."

Fat Henry said, "Yeah, come back, faggots." He looked at Matt and said, "Nice hair, ya fucking homo. Where'd you get that done? A salon?" He said, "I love the little kitty cat on your arm. My girlfriend has the same tattoo, you fucking dick sucker."

I said, "Fuck you, fat ass."

Matt said, "Yeah, fuck you, dickless," then we bolted through the door and down the stairs and to the Nova while Fat Henry lunged and missed.

I thought he would follow, thought he would turn his fatness into a torpedo and destroy us, but when I turned around he was on the porch, leaning on the railing with both hands like he was trying to collapse the wood. We opened our doors and Matt started the engine and I stood there and flipped Fat Henry off.

I said, "Fuck off, fatso."

Fat Henry nodded, but he knew. It was the booze. It was the drugs. It was Charlie Chan standing inside with his jujitsu skills. You didn't kill paying customers this early in the day. Fat Henry pointed at me like his finger was a knife but he turned and walked back into the trailer.

Matt said, "Let's fucking go," and revved the Nova. He whipped it around, and we didn't look back, the potholes and dirt piles making the car bounce like a rabbit.

CHAPTER 43

Duke's Bar in Ligonier was a fine working-man's bar. It was nicer than Al's Tavern. There was a dartboard and a pool table, bowling, a payphone, a jukebox that played CDs. I hadn't been carded. The man at the front door asked Matt for ID and Matt produced his neighbor's license and said, "I let the hair grow in a little."

The bouncer said, "I'll say," and let him pass.

I had a beer in front of me. Matt had a beer in front of him. The baggies of coke were in our pockets, and we had planned to take turns in the restroom, but now it was quiet and we were barely drinking. Everything should have been a celebration, but it was the opposite of that. There was Fat Henry and what he'd said and nothing else.

I was a dick sucker. Matt had homo hair styled at a salon. Getting smashed would have been fine, like the names were fine, but Fat Henry had insulted our tattoos before we had even shown them to the world, before we had even studied them ourselves, and now we had to wear them for the rest of our lives. My faggoty little rose. Matt's gay little cat.

That motherfucker, I thought, and I had to stop myself from crying.

Matt said, "You okay?" and I couldn't answer.

The bartender came back and Matt ordered wings and a basket of fries.

I asked for a glass of water. It felt like surrender, a white flag going up a pole.

I said, "I have to piss."

I went to the restroom and stood in front of the mirror. My shirt was on, so I pulled up the sleeve.

I flexed my arm. I flexed it again. I looked away then back. It was a tattoo, but I didn't know if it was cool anymore. I tried another angle. I touched the tender skin. Of course it was cool. Other people would think so too, but Fat Henry had the loudest voice, and it said, "That tattoo is gay." It said, "You are nothing." It said, "Quit now." It was an echo, and I didn't know I could pulverize it with a couple more lines and a few more beers. I stood there, depressed, strung out. I rubbed my tricep and looked at my shoulder and the way the tattoo was still slightly swollen and bloody, and I did my best to love it

I went back to the bar.

I said, "Fuck Fat Henry."

Matt said, "I don't know."

After that, we ate wings. The wings were hot and made us thirsty. We drank our warm beers and ordered new cold ones. We ate more. We drank more. I went back to the restroom and found my little bag of drugs. I did my best to smash up a tiny rock on the toilet paper dispenser. I did a long chunky line with a dollar bill. I left a line for Matt, and he came back smiling. We quit the wings. We ordered more beer. We did another line.

I said, "Seriously, fuck Fat Henry."

Matt said, "Okay, fuck that guy," but he looked at his panther and touched it with his hand like he was erasing the design.

Skee-ball was the ticket. Once we started that, our drinking doubled, and we had to slow down our trips to the bathroom so it wouldn't be obvious. We moved to the bowling game. Nobody was in the bar now except the bouncer and the bartender, but it felt like a full house. Things had happened. But we weren't done.

And so we were ready when Fat Henry stumbled through the door.

The bartender, the bouncer, even the bar itself, was ready.

The bartender said, "Henry, get out. We said June. Keep your nose clean, and you can come back for summer. That was the deal." He said, "Now beat it before I call the cops."

Fat Henry was barely conscious. He was fatter and sweatier and, up close, probably stinkier. He couldn't speak or even focus his eyes. I thought he might tip over, but he leaned into the doorframe. It was a hard lean, full of gravity and hate. The side of his head bounced off the wood. He wiped his nose and tried to focus on the bartender who was still pointing away from the bar. I looked for a new tattoo, but there were so many it was impossible to tell. He was, I'm sure, on dope, but I didn't know what dope was, so I figured he had chugged a bottle of Jack Daniels or inhaled a case of beer in twenty-four sips.

The bouncer said, "Okay, Henry, time to go."

The bouncer was large but clean-cut, with short brown hair and nice pressed blue jeans and a yellow golf shirt. Henry didn't move. I rolled the ball down the lane to see if he would look our way, but he didn't.

Matt picked up the small bowling ball we'd been rolling and mouthed, "It's him."

I said, "I know it's him."

Fat Henry said, "Fuck you, Bill," to the old-man bartender, then he waved everything off and moved through the door like his legs were stumps.

Bill said, "Yeah, fuck me," and sort of fake-laughed and walked through a swinging metal door to the backroom or the kitchen.

The bouncer, who had never moved from his stool, finally looked up and smiled. He said, "What an asshole." Then he moved towards the back.

Matt said, "I don't think he saw us."

I said, "Good."

Matt picked up a bowling pin. It was small and wood, maybe the size of a Pepsi bottle. I picked up another pin and we moved through the bar and out the door. It was evening now, and the parking lights blurred the night. The cocaine had lifted me, but I thought it was confidence. I thought it was bravery. I felt drunk and strong.

Matt said, "There he is," and pointed across the parking lot with his bowling pin.

Henry rested on his car, a huge Oldsmobile. It was a tank, covered in nicks and dents. The back panels were mismatched and one of the fenders had rusted down. The driver's side door was open. The engine was off. Henry was standing but bent, his head on the roof like he might throw up on his own black leather railroad boots.

Matt said, "He's mine," but he didn't move.

I said, "Me first," and started to jog at Fat Henry who heard my footsteps and looked up as I cocked back my bowling pin and said, "Who's the faggot now, Henry?"

CHAPTER 44

In the moment after I hit Fat Henry and Fat Henry dropped but did not disappear, it ended for Matt. The bowling pin was in my hand. Henry had fallen into his car then out again, bouncing off the steering wheel then the inside of the door, then down to one knee on the asphalt of the parking lot. I had wanted to kill him, but I missed. What had looked like his head in the darkness was his shoulder or his arm or some fleshy spot with tattoos, and not his skull.

He said, "You fuckers!" and I wanted to hit him again, knew that he would kill me if I didn't hit him again, that if he found his balance and his legs and remembered how to work the knuckles in his hands, he would kill me, a punch, a choke, a kick, he'd stop my breath. But when I raised the pin, I stepped back and held it there. Henry lunged for my legs, diving from his knees to his face, his chin crashing the pavement.

I said, "Try again, you fucker," but I didn't want him to. I wanted him to fall into the parking lot like it was tar, to drown there. I wanted him to pass out and forget, to go where evil drunks go and not come back. He lived like a weapon. I'd never seen a person live like a weapon. I couldn't kill him. He couldn't be killed. The vibrations from the first shot with the bowling pin, wood on muscle, wood on fat and bone, rang my arm like a telephone, and now I didn't know if I could make a fist. I didn't want to make a fist.

Henry crawled on his stomach. He was bleeding. Tiny rocks and scabs filled out his beard like berries in a shrub. He rocked from his belly to his knees. He did it again, righting himself, sitting back on his legs like a cripple, still a giant but barely off the ground.

Matt touched my wrist. He lowered my arm.

He said, "Come on."

I looked at his hand. His bowling pin was gone. It was back by the entrance to Duke's Bar. He hadn't intended to club anyone.

Matt said, "Let's go. He's done."

Henry was done. I wanted to go. I raised my bowling pin again.

Henry said, "Fucking use it." He was more sober than before, as sober as someone could be who had not been sober in days. The violence had shifted his brain and he remembered how to speak, how to threaten.

I said, "I will."

He said, "It's my pleasure."

I said, "Crawl over here, you fucking slug."

Matt said, "Just fuck that fag," but barely, and he motioned towards the Nova.

Henry said, "I'm the fag?" He said, "I'm the fag with the fag tattoos?" He leaned forward and spit a web of blood into his hand. He pulled at the blood like it was a rag someone had stuffed down his throat. He stopped and gagged. He tried to throw up, but it was dry. He wiped the blood on his sweatpants, on his Steelers' shirt. He looked at Matt and pointed with his bloody fingers and said, "There you are, Vidal Sassoon. How you doing?"

Matt said, "Come on."

Henry said, "What about it, fag? You gonna beat me up with that hair-do?"

Matt said, "The cops are gonna come."

Matt didn't talk to Henry. He talked to me, and I talked to Henry.

I said, "Henry, shut the fuck up."

Matt said, "Seriously, cops. Think about it."

Henry said, "You wish the cops would come, you pussy-whip." He said, "Where's Charlie Chan, that gook wanna-be?"

I said, "Enough."

Henry didn't look at me.

He looked at Matt.

He said, "Hey, Lita Ford, you gonna take a shot?"

He said, "Your friend do all your dirty work, you cunt?"

He said, "Exactly what I figured," and he spat at Matt and the spit rolled out of Henry's mouth like a flat tire and down his chin and onto his clothes.

He said, "Fuck me."

He said, "Hair-do, you know what prison is like, rapeface?"

Then I kicked him.

I moved in with the bowling pin, but I couldn't, so I raised my foot and stomped Henry in the chest, and he tipped back like a door falling off its hinges.

"There," I said, like it meant something, and I moved to the Nova.

I held the bowling pin so my fingerprints couldn't be traced, and Henry could keep the tread on my shoes, right there, on his fat chest.

CHAPTER 45

Matt drove the Nova like a space ship, weaving through traffic like we weren't on wheels. He was crying. I pretended he wasn't. The bowling pin was in my lap. It was dark, but I turned it and looked for blood. There wasn't any. Matt blew through two yellow lights and finally stopped at a red. He was making sounds now, the moans and coughs and snorts that Susan had made after the clinic and the pregnancy test, when she turned her insides out at Burger King.

I said, "Take it easy." I said, "You want me to drive?"

He said, "Yes." He said, "No." He said, "It's my car." He lifted his t-shirt at the waist and covered his nose and blew out all the snot. He said, "I'm disgusting. I hate myself."

The light turned green. Matt punched it.

I said, "If you're worried about cops, slow down."

Matt said, "I'm not worried about cops." He wiped his nose with his elbow, his skin. He said, "I'm worried about me." He said, "I should just kill Susan, that's what I should do."

I said, "You shouldn't do that."

He said, "I should. I should kill her. Poison, gun, whatever."

He was serious. But I'd been serious about killing Henry, and now I wasn't.

He said, "It'd be easy."

I said, "Yeah," but I was thinking about my own plans.

193

If he wanted to kill Susan, he might want to kill himself. He might want to kill me. He might want to turn this car into a bullet and fire us at another car coming head on.

But then he should have killed Henry. But then he should have used the bowling pin. There were people to kill. Susan was not one of them. Susan was not even Susan if there was a baby growing inside her. I didn't want to die in a Nova with a guy who wanted to kill his pregnant girlfriend, with someone who let Fat Henry call him a cunt.

I said, "Pull over."

He said, "Can't."

I said, "Pull over."

He turned and looked at me and pushed his hair out of his face and said, "What if I don't fucking want to?"

I said, "Then I'll punch you."

He said, "I knew you'd say that." He said, "You're my best friend, and you say that." He said, "Great." He said, "Thanks a fucking lot."

I turned towards the window.

He said, "I will. I'll pull over as soon as I can get off this highway." He said this through tears, staring ahead, waiting for another road.

He slowed down to the speed limit. He caught his breath and lost it and caught it again.

He said, "You can punch me. It wouldn't do anything."

I said, "I don't want to punch you."

He said, "Maybe it would help."

I said, "It wouldn't."

He said, "Then don't punch me." He said, "I want to kill Susan. I don't see how anyone could say this is my fault. Like a jury of my peers would ever convict me."

He stopped at another red light. We were three cars back. There was a gas station with a dozen different banners advertising tobacco. There was a beer distributor. Beyond that, a mini golf course and a go-cart track.

Matt said, "I'll never drink again."

I said, "Sure you will." I said, "We'll wake up tomorrow and this will be better."

He said, "It won't. I've been kidding myself. It's gonna get worse."

The light went green. Before anyone could move, Matt pounded the horn. Then he took his head and threw it like a baseball against the side window. The thud was deep, like a hammer on a hollow wall, but the glass didn't break.

I said, "Easy."

He smashed his head again, two times, short bursts.

He said, "I'm fine," and raised both hands like he was surrendering. He said, "Okay."

All the cars had moved. Behind us, someone lightly tooted a horn.

We pulled into my driveway.

Matt said, "I'll call you."

I said, "When?"

He said, "When I'm better."

CHAPTER 46

He wasn't going to get better.

While I went inside my house and threw up in the bathroom, and said to my mom through a locked door, "I got the flu today when I was studying," Matt went home and hid in the detached garage out back.

Matt's dad was away somewhere, working on a roof, drinking in a bar, somewhere.

Matt's mom was home, but she was tired. She'd been at her catering business since three in the morning, making lasagnas for a three-hundred-seat wedding. She'd never done a wedding this size before, and she still didn't know how she was going to bake thirty sheets of lasagna and keep them all hot at the same time. When she'd arrived home at six o'clock, she had a glass of wine and turned the TV on in her bedroom. She immediately fell asleep. She woke up once at midnight to kick off her clothes and didn't wake up again until her alarm sounded the next day. It was still dark out. She knew her kids were fine, and she didn't want to wake them anyway, so she grabbed a diet Pepsi and went back to the catering business and the lasagnas.

Matt heard her car leave the driveway. He hadn't slept. Sleeping was impossible. He had some cocaine left, and he did that. He thought about Susan. He didn't love her anymore. He probably hated her. Maybe he still loved her, but not like he had before. His parents had said he was too young to be dating so seriously. He didn't want to kill Susan anymore, but he didn't want to have a baby with her or help her abort the baby or anything that had to do with anything. He wanted to play rock n' roll, but everyone wanted to play rock n' roll.

When he was sure his mom was gone, he went inside the house and poured a glass of wine from the open bottle. He didn't know if he could get drunk anymore. He'd been up for over twenty-four hours. He'd been sober and drunk, thrown up, taken pills, gotten tattooed and almost cried like a girl. He'd done cocaine for the first time and loved it. Then hated it. He'd been happy in a bar and miserable in a bar. He'd been called a cunt and a fag and everything else by a three-hundred-pound psycho redneck nazi, and he'd done nothing about it. The best thing Matt had done was hate himself. His best friend had saved his life, had beat down Fat Henry, and Matt had thought about killing his best friend, smashing them both into a tree or a brick building at ninety miles an hour. Matt hated everyone. It would be impossible to kill everyone he hated, and besides the people he hated were also the ones he loved.

He took the bottle of wine into his dad's office and found a pencil and some paper. Then he found his dad's shotgun, the one he hunted squirrel with. He went back out to the detached garage and started his suicide note.

What I've told you so far—the recounting of the day, Matt's desire to kill everyone he loved—was in his first draft, crumpled in a ball on the garage floor.

A later version, found near the body, was more generous.

CHAPTER 47

The phone rang and the answering machine picked up. I waited. It could have been the school. It didn't matter. My mom knew I was home. I had the flu. I hadn't been to school in days. I hadn't heard from Matt. Matt was off somewhere, being himself, crying I assumed, thinking about killing his girlfriend and not fighting Fat Henry. I didn't really have the flu. I was hungover. My hangover wouldn't go away. My heart wouldn't slow down. Or it slowed down then sped up when I pushed my fingers into my ears and listened for a beat.

I had been watching Andy Griffith reruns on TV. There was Opie and Andy and Barney and Aunt May. The kid was nice. The sheriff was smart and compassionate. His sidekick was a bumbling idiot, but he was loveable and treated the town drunk with respect. The aunt was fat and funny and had all the answers. I couldn't get enough of "The Andy Griffith Show," watching episode after episode on channel 53, while I ate bowl after bowl of cereal.

It was a woman on the answering machine, and she was talking about blinds. At first I thought she was talking about people who couldn't see, then I realized she was talking about blinds, like drapes. Then I realized it was Susan. I didn't want to talk to Susan. I didn't want to think about Susan. She had probably talked to Matt. I would have to talk to Susan about Susan or Matt or both, and I mainly wanted to focus on Andy Griffith and Opie and the fishing trip they were about to go on.

The voice said, "Hello, this is Susan from JC Penney's and I'm calling today about a great offer on some blind treatments." She said, "Our blinds have never been priced this low. If you were home, I could explain."

I picked up the phone and said, "Blinds?"

She said, "Mr. Charles?"

I said, "Hey Susan, what's up?"

She said, "Danny." She said, "I'm trying to find you." She said, "God," and it sounded desperate and loving like she'd been roaming the world, searching for me.

I said, "I'm sick. I think I have the flu."

She said, "Have you seen Matt?"

I said, "I guess he's at school." I said, "Where are you?"

She said, "I came home. I don't know where Matt is. He's been gone for days. His mom's in Ohio at some wedding, and his dad's somewhere working, and no one knows where he is. I hoped he was with you." She said, "I'm mad at him." She said, "He's a real asshole.

I said, "Don't be mad at him." I said, "He's not an asshole."

Susan said, "Danny?"

I said, "Yeah?"

I said, "I'm awful. My grandma picked me up from school and dropped me off so she could run and get some medicine and now I'm all alone." She said, "I hate being alone. Matt knows that. He knows it, and he does it to me anyway." She said, "My parents are at work. I'm upstairs in my bedroom. I don't have anyone to talk to and all I want to do is talk. I have to talk."

I said, "Oh." I wanted to punch Susan, more than Matt. They were both damaged. They were damaging me with what they'd done. I'd damaged myself.

She said, "I can't stop thinking about that test." She said, "You have to come over or I don't know what I'll do."

I said, "Your grandma will be back with the medicine."

Susan said, "And she'll leave again, and both my parents are gone until late tonight." She said, "I don't know where Matt is." She said, "I know he's your best friend, but I hate him. I've hated him for a long time. He's stupid and an alcoholic, just like his dad."

I said, "Matt's not stupid."

She said, "He is." She said, "And he cries, and I hate it. He cries like a baby when he's with me, and he acts tough when he's with you."

I said, "I don't have a car."

Susan said, "There's an extra car here. I'll come and get you."

I said, "My mind is fried from drugs," and I meant it, but I also meant that more drugs might be the solution to saving my mind from drugs.

Susan said, "I don't care." She said, "My mom has a medicine cabinet filled with bottles. You can have whatever you want." She said, "Danny, please."

I said, "No." I said, "I can't." I said, "It's impossible."

And then I did. I walked out the backdoor and through the woods and towards the Norwin Auction, and I sat on a rusted bulldozer and waited where it looked like they had started to build something and then stopped.

CHAPTER 48

Susan's tongue was in my mouth. Her hands were in my hair, and I was squeezing her ass, mostly because I was taller and she was falling into me. We were upstairs, in the bathroom.

Susan pulled back. She said, "We can't." She said, "We shouldn't be doing this," and when I didn't agree or disagree, she lunged at me with her mouth.

Then she stopped and said my name like it was a command.

I wanted to hide in a towel. I wanted to crawl into the bathtub, even without the water.

Susan said, "Danny," but she was kissing me again, her tongue deep in my mouth.

My lips were very sensitive, except they were also very numb.

I closed my eyes. I opened my eyes.

The bathroom was pink, like it had been painted for a princess. The sink and toilet and tub were all pink. The cabinets were brown but the handles were pink. The tissues in the purple Kleenex box were pink. The towels were pink, fluffy. My face was pink. I felt it.

I said, "What's up with all this pink?"

Susan said, "I don't know."

I said, "I thought your mom was trying to kill this stuff, pink and cheerleaders."

Susan said, "My mom was a cheerleader."

I said, "But you can't be a cheerleader?"

I wanted to fuck Susan so bad, I didn't want to fuck her. I wanted to talk about pink things and cheerleaders and female lawyers.

Susan said, "I don't want to be a cheerleader. It's stupid and mean."

Susan's lips matched the bathroom. They were a color not found in nature, and it looked good on her. She didn't notice how embarrassed I was, or she didn't care.

Susan said, "The talk is ruining it." She said, "I like to talk afterward."

She kissed me. I pretended to be confused. I only kissed back when I had to.

Then I slid my hands down the back of her jeans. It felt exactly like the pictures I'd seen, the Polaroids, the naked ones, only better, only softer.

She kissed the side of my mouth.

She said, "I'm wet."

She kissed my neck and ears and even my nipples as she pulled my shirt over my head, right before I helped with the buttons on her jeans.

CHAPTER 49

Susan was on her knees in the bathroom. She was touching herself. I was behind her, trying to keep up. There was a long mirror on the door, and I kept glancing at my tattoo. I hated how my rose fit in here. It was like my shoulder had been decorated. My tattoo could have been on a towel or a shower curtain or a fuzzy rug. I wanted Susan to say she loved my tattoo. But she couldn't see my tattoo. Her face was on the floor.

"I just need it," Susan said. "Do you need it?"

I didn't say anything.

I tried to show her with my body.

"Thank you," Susan said. She liked the talking after but she wouldn't stop talking during. She said, "I knew you'd come. I knew you'd come to be with me." She said, "You deserve this." She said, "Thank you, thank you. You deserve this."

I deserved something, not this. I felt like I could come, but I slowed down. Then I tried to speed up and get it back, but it was gone, disappeared back inside my body. I'd never had sex with a pregnant girl before, and it was making me sick.

Susan said, "It's been so long." She said, "Don't you feel like you need it?" She said, "I know you need this, Danny, I know you do."

I said, "I do," but I didn't. I always wanted it, and I hadn't ever turned it down, but it always felt like a gift or a luxury, like a vacation, not a need, not like shelter and food. But Susan needed it. It was essential. It was a place to live. I believed her when she talked.

Susan said, "Matt doesn't fuck me anymore." She said, "He hates me." She said, "I hate him more."

She said, "I wanted him to fuck me like this, but he wouldn't."

I was sweating too much to be sexy. I was dripping everywhere. The floor was wet. There were tiny puddles, raindrops touching raindrops.

Susan said, "This is what I wanted."

I moved my arm so my tattoo was there if she turned back. If I pulled her hair, she'd have to see my tattoo in the mirror. But maybe she'd seen it. Maybe it was too terrible to mention. I turned my arm another way and flexed.

Susan said, "Matt doesn't do this." She said, "He won't, he won't."

My legs ached. I'd never fucked on a tile floor. Susan didn't mind. She moved like she was on a bed, something soft. I tried but it was my knees. I moved like I was on a tile floor.

I shifted to get a better angle then, mid-shift, I slipped and almost kicked her in the face. She moved, lunged forward. She collapsed flat on her belly. Before I could get my hands down, I landed on her back with my chest. We bounced. It was a wrestling move. It made sounds. The sounds were the floor and Susan's body and then her voice. I could have crushed her. It could have been her head. I sat back up. She turned around. She was okay, but scared, like I'd done it on purpose.

She said, "I'm sorry." She said, "That was hateful. Matt's your best friend. I shouldn't have said that." She said, "I shouldn't be mentioning his name."

I said, "I just slipped on my sweat."

She said, "Don't hate me."

I said, "I don't hate you."

She said, "Everyone hates me."

I said, "I don't."
She moved back to her knees.
I moved back to mine.

CHAPTER 50

I finished and Susan said, "We should get dressed."

I said, "We should."

I made sure I didn't fall when I got up from the floor.

Susan didn't look at me. She pulled on her panties and bra and socks from the floor, reaching out for a piece of clothing when she needed it.

I did my underwear first, then my t-shirt. I'd never felt so naked. Being naked felt awful.

Susan said, "I'm glad Matt's gone."

I said, "Yeah." I said, "I wish I knew where he was though."

She said, "I don't."

She turned and crawled a few steps for the rest of her clothes. I sat down on the toilet. It was a big bathroom. There were two sinks, two mirrors.

If she was pregnant already, it didn't matter that I came inside her.

My feet and legs were too sweaty to pull on my socks, so I stood and put them in my front pockets, one sock in each. Susan bunched the rest of her clothes in a pile and walked out of the bathroom and down the hall. I hurried up. When she came back, I was dressed, and she was in pajamas, red flannel ones with pink hearts, and white tennis shoes.

She said, "I'm going to tell you everything, okay?"

I said, "Maybe you shouldn't."

She said, "I have to."

I said, "But maybe you shouldn't."

She said, "It's not fair what I've done to you. You don't owe me anything, and you've been doing everything. Matt hasn't done anything. I'm sorry, but he hasn't."

I said, "Okay."

She said, "I'm getting an abortion on Saturday."

I said, "This Saturday?"

It was this Saturday. She was done with everything else. She'd called the clinic. She didn't care about the blood test. Even if the blood test came back negative, it would be a lie. Susan was pregnant.

She said, "I can feel it inside me. It's swimming like a fish." She said, "It's already trying to get out. I have to stop it."

I said, "But this Saturday?"

She said, "Are you hearing me?"

She had an appointment. She knew the doctor's name. There were programs that would help her pay, but she wouldn't use those programs. Those programs wanted real names and ages and social security numbers.

She said, "Matt has all the money I stole."

I said, "I know."

I didn't say I was wearing her money, that I'd drunk it and snorted it, too.

I said, "I thought there was more money."

She said, "I made that up." She said, "I wanted Matt to think my mom was saving up to leave my dad, but there wasn't any money. That was my life savings."

I said, "Two hundred and fifty dollars?"

She said, "So." She said, "What's your life savings?" Her face was like a bomb that was about to explode. She said, "We do the paint store tonight."

CHAPTER 51

There was a gun somewhere. Susan said so. It was part of her plan. We were up in the attic. She wasn't listening to me. We were getting the gun. It was probably two o'clock.

The attic was dusty. It was dark and hard to breathe. The only light was a bulb hanging from the ceiling. It was an awful attic for a family that had two lawyers in the house. Wood beams were exposed. I reached to brace myself and felt the rot, the dry crumbling wood. Long strips of pink insulation were unrolling from the inside of the roof. Everything was in boxes, stacked, and the boxes were collapsing in on themselves.

I looked in the corner for some money, a stack of it, a bucket of change, but there were sweaters in a ripped-up garbage bag and a pile of old lamps, the cords tangled into a knot.

Susan said, "My dad needs to do something or get someone in here to fix this." She said, "This is pathetic. Someone needs to clean this out."

I said, "We're never going to find this gun."

She said, "We have to find it."

I couldn't see where to step and it was possible Susan wanted to shoot me, but at least I was dressed and my sweaty hair had started to dry and I wasn't having sex with my best friend's girlfriend anymore.

Susan said, "We don't have to talk about Matt anymore. That part is over."

I said, "I didn't say anything about Matt."

She said, "You were thinking it."

I said, "It's dark."

Susan said, "Do you have a flashlight?"

I said, "Do I look like I have a flashlight?"

She said, "Help me look for one."

She went back to the boxes. Most of the boxes were cardboard. I could see some wood crates. A wood crate was a good place to store a gun.

I said, "Let's think again." I said, "You should wait for the blood test."

She said, "I told you. It's in there. I need it out." She said, "I have my appointment. If I don't do it now, I won't do it. Matt will show up, and he'll propose to me, and we'll sneak off to some hillbilly state and get married." She said, "Having Matt would be like having two babies."

I hated Susan, really hated her.

I was going to do whatever she wanted.

She said, "It's back here somewhere," and moved towards the crates. She said, "My mom wouldn't let my dad keep it downstairs, but he shoots crows from the back porch sometimes."

I said, "Matt wasn't going to use a gun."

She said, "I'm not Matt."

She was opening boxes now.

I said, "I don't know what he was going to do. Pretend he had a gun maybe. But he definitely wasn't going to use a gun. He doesn't even have a gun."

"His dad does."

"Matt's not his dad."

"But he is," Susan said.

I said, "The woman who drops the money is old and scared. You tell her to hand it over, and she'll hand it over."

Susan said, "I'm not doing it without a gun."

"Don't do it then," I said.

Susan stopped searching. She pulled her hair back into a ponytail then let it fall. I could see the trunk she'd been digging through. She closed the lid. She covered the trunk with an old sheet. She sat down on the floor and leaned against a mattress that leaned against a wall. She combed her hair over her face with her fingers so I couldn't see anything, her eyes or mouth or nose, nothing. It was creepy and weird, like she was a little monster, or almost a monster, turning.

I wanted to pull the mattress down. I wondered how they got such a large mattress through such a small attic door. I wondered what Susan would look like underneath the mattress.

She said, "What?"

I said, "Nothing. I'm looking. I'm just thinking."

She said, "Look at yourself," and pulled some more at her hair.

I sat down. I didn't know if the floor was safe.

Susan said, "Do you want to help me or not?"

I thought she could see me, but not what I was doing. I shook my head no.

She said, "Just say you won't if you won't."

I said, "I will." I said, "But no gun."

She said, "I need the gun."

I said, "You do not need a gun."

She said, "No bullets. Maybe I didn't mention that before. I wasn't going to load the gun. I don't even know how."

I said, "I don't believe you."

She said, "I think he hides the bullets somewhere else." She said, "My dad is smart like that, despite what you've heard." She said, "No bullets. She said, "I swear."

CHAPTER 52

Marjorie, who had the money bag, didn't move. The bag looked lost in her hands, bigger than a wallet but smaller than a purse, the wrong size for anything. Marjorie put her fingers on the zipper and touched the teeth like she was petting something. She stepped back. She pulled the bag close to her chest, like something precious, like it was a pet, a child.

Susan took another step at Marjorie and said, "Just drop the bag and walk away."

Susan had shown up at ten o'clock, dressed in jeans and a bulky sweatshirt, her hair pulled back inside the hood, her face partially covered with a red bandana. When we'd turned the corner, she was there, looking like a man, a thug. She was thick and low to the ground. When she talked, she sounded like a guy trying to disguise his voice.

She was Matt, but more.

She said, "The money." She said, "Now," and made a motion with her left hand.

The gun was in her right hand, hanging at her side. Her voice was a growl, like it'd gone through something and been shredded.

Susan said, "The money. Let's go."

I didn't have the money bag so I didn't go. I stood. I waited. I adjusted my tie. It was a new one, red with tiny diamonds. I wore my dress cords. My nametag was shined, the angle straight, not falling. I felt professional and mature, not like a thief, not like someone who'd watch an innocent person get shot.

Work had been great. I'd helped customers. I'd matched paint colors and mixed up gallons and quarts. The dustpan had disappeared, so I swept the floors and picked up the dirt with a piece of cardboard. I wasn't hungover. I wasn't sick. The old cans and buckets in the back that needed to go to the dumpster, I did that.

If Susan were Matt, I would have called and said, "Not tonight," and cancelled the robbery. I would have said, "Next week," or, "Two weeks," or, "Never."

But Susan was Susan, not waiting for my call, not listening to my plans.

Susan was home, loading her pistol.

Susan said there wouldn't be bullets.

There were bullets.

Now she said, "The money, let's go."

Marjorie neither dropped the bag, nor walked away. She stood. I watched her face but it was a wall, not even a blink. She could have been having a heart attack or a stroke or been struck by paralysis. I wanted to touch her, to take the bag, but I thought she would collapse.

Susan moved the gun, just a little, a quick point from her hip.

I was more scared than if this had been a real robbery. During a real robbery, I would have known what to do, fight or run or drop to my knees and beg.

I said, "Marjorie, just give him the money," making sure I used the male pronoun.

Marjorie didn't say anything. She looked old, ancient. She looked like a woman who had just discovered how to turn style and design and fashion into violence but on accident. Her wrinkles and the few gray hairs around her ears had turned against her. Even her wrists, crossed over the money bag, looked brittle.

Before we'd left the store, she'd asked where my jacket was. She was worried. It could be cold. She wore a heavy coat and it was spring.

All she had to do was drop the bag.

She turned towards me. I motioned that she should hand over the money.

I said, "Go ahead. Just give it to her."

Susan looked over her shoulder. I didn't know where she'd parked. Her plan was her gun. I hoped she had a full tank of gas and an escape route.

Susan looked at Marjorie. Marjorie tried to cough, to speak, to clear her throat.

I said, "Don't worry about it, Marjorie."

Cars came and went, but that was Route 30, off in the distance. In the plaza, the lights were dim. The long skinny bulbs above us buzzed. All the stores were closed. The pizza place was empty. The windows were glass, and the curtains pulled back. There was a safe in there. I'd seen the owner on his knees. He turned the dial. There were bags of money. There were little slips of paper. He didn't believe in banks. He talked about being rich. I should have gone in at night with a crow bar. A crow bar was safer than a loaded pistol.

Susan said, "Let's go now," and her voice was deeper and huskier and manlier.

Marjorie said, "But," and she stuttered on the last few beats. She said, "But why?"

The fears that went along with working in a paint store included negligent bosses, cash registers that didn't balance, and colors that dried too dark. Once, in the parking lot, as she was getting into her car, Marjorie said, "I forgot to lock the file cabinet," and put her hand to her mouth like she'd lost a child in the city. Another time, Marjorie lent a wallpaper book to a customer without getting the customer's name, and when I found her in the office, she was in tears. Marjorie was scared of many things, and she believed in god, and she went to church, and she spoke poorly of herself when she missed mass, and she worried about the weather, that the cold might sicken us all, and none of those things were guns or had prepared her for a gun.

I said, "Marjorie, give him the money."

I said, "Marjorie, that's all he wants."

I said, "Marjorie, please."

I reached to take the bag from her. I moved slowly. If she wouldn't let go, I would tug at the bag or knock it to the ground. I looked at Susan. I needed a minute. Susan looked at Marjorie. I could see Susan's arm, the one that held the gun, and how it was anxious.

A hundred feet away, in the parking lot, a car door slammed and the engine turned over.

Susan raised the gun from her side and pointed it at Marjorie. It was so fast, I thought she'd fired, that there was a silencer, that the sound had blown away. Marjorie said god's name and closed her eyes, the bag still tight against her chest, bunched up with her jacket. I looked for blood. I breathed. No one was shot. As long as that, we were okay.

Susan shook the gun, poked it through the air, pointing, aiming.

I stepped to Marjorie, in front of Marjorie. I put my hand in the air.

I looked at Susan and said, "Don't!" I said, "Hold on!" I was in front of the gun now.

Susan held the pistol. Her arm moved like a tree branch in the storm, like she was aiming at me, then over me at Marjorie, the wind deciding.

I pulled my voice back and said, "Just calm down. Be calm." I said, "Don't do that."

I turned to face Marjorie, who looked like a child, who had fallen into herself, and said, "Give him the bag. Give him the bag, so we can go home, that's all. Just give him the bag."

Marjorie sidestepped me. She was slow and crippled. One step took three. Susan moved at Marjorie, fast. I was alone, two steps away. I wasn't going to get shot. Susan extended her arm. I looked at the gun. It was so real, it did not look real, just like Susan did not look like a man anymore but like Susan dressed in a sweatshirt with her long hair falling out.

Marjorie said, "I have to leave." She said, "I have to walk away now."

Susan said, "Don't move."

Marjorie said, "I don't want this."

Susan said, "Stop." She said, "Now." She braced her arm with her other hand.

Marjorie took another tiny step and said, "I have to go home."

Susan said, "You can't." She said, "You can't, you can't," her voice going back, sounding girlish and scared. She raised the pistol from Marjorie's chest.

Then she pointed up, and fired.

Dave Newman lives and writes in Trafford, Pennsylvania.

Visit: www.davenewmanwritesbooks.com

ALSO FROM WORLD PARADE BOOKS:

Poetry:

Gerald Locklin: New and Selected Poems
        By Gerald Locklin
The Cézanne/Pissarro Poems
        By Gerald Locklin
The Green Season
        By Donna Hilbert
The Womb of Memory
        By Dibakar Barua
All the Poets Who Have Touched Me/Desire
        By Lyn Lifshin
Growing Up in Someone Else's Shoes
        By Sam Pierstorff
Witness
        By Elizabeth Young
Tao Driver and Selected Poems
        By Rafael Zepeda
And Through the Woods
        By Ron Koertge
Beside the City of Angels:
An Anthology of Long Beach Poetry
        Edited By Paul Kareem Tayyar
Stop
        By Kevin Lee
Horizon's Pocket
        By Regina Nervo
Dancing Under a River of Stars
        By Joan Jobe Smith

Fiction

The Vampires Saved Civilization: New and Selected
Prose, 2000-2010
    By Gerald Locklin
Orphans (Forthcoming 2010)
    By Barry Spacks
The Office (Forthcoming 2010)
    By Edward Field
The Sophomore (Forthcoming 2010)
    By Barry Spacks

Memoir

Kabuli Days: Travels in Old Afghanistan
    By Edward Field
Where We Live
    By LeeAnne Langton

Young Adult

The Macki-Bald Inn
    By E.A. Day

28013253R00119

Made in the USA
Lexington, KY
02 December 2013